METAL

A Mickey Crow Paranormal Adventure

Gevera Bert Piedmont

Published by
Transformations by Obsidian Butterfly LLC
Yalesville CT USA
ObsidianButterfly.com

ISBN: 978-1-963760-07-1

Cover composite by Gevera Bert Piedmont
Cover images from Freepik and Pixabay
Author photo copyright 2021 by Ayzha Wolf Photography

When Robots Get Angry, Things get METAL

"Murderbot meets Supernatural"

One-armed Mickey Crow, reluctant socialite Pris, and mad scientist Mo take a break from the Contrary Crowcast and monster hunting to spend a few relaxing days at Unieda Corporation playing with bots. Their friends Geoffrey and Taylor are pitting their pair of Giant Golden Gear-winning rumble robots against Unieda's new all-purpose spidogs, a trio of metal spider-dog hybrids.

Unieda Corporation has ulterior motives in inviting Mickey to this robot extravaganza, however, and she's not happy to discover she's a test subject more than a guest.

Then the robot rumble goes sideways, an old enemy appears, and things get METAL.

Contains spoilers for the first two Mickey Crow adventure, Shiver *and* Formless, *available from Amazon in paperback or Kindle Unlimited.*

METAL

A Mickey Crow
Paranormal Adventure
by
Gevera Bert Piedmont

-1-
Mickey

"What do you mean she's not on the approved guest list?" Mickey Crow leaned across Pris to yell at the flustered woman in charge of the front gate at the Unieda Corporation gate, just outside of Boston.

"There is no Priscilla Salamanca listed for today."

"So, I'm on there, but not Pris."

The seatbelt chime dinged, and Pris's pale face loomed close to Mickey's left cheek.

"Look, Geoffrey and Taylor Chu invited us here today. We didn't just randomly show up."

The woman stared into Pris's car, mouth scrunched, clearly thinking she wasn't paid enough for this. "I'll make a call. Pull over there."

Mickey flung herself back into the passenger seat and tucked the stump of her left arm into her side. She didn't put on her seatbelt. The dinging continued.

They waited in the small parking lot outside the enormous Unieda campus, a well-manicured space with retaining ponds, gardens, autumn-colored trees, a forest of solar panels, and half a dozen scattered buildings connected by corridors, all surrounded by an aggressive amount of security fencing.

"I just want my arm back." Mickey bounced in the leather seat in time with the chime. "And I want to harass your car while we're driving."

"My car doesn't appreciate that. I was hoping they would fix that glitch."

"But then I might not be able to work with Ek anymore. I miss Ek." Ek had started out as a bird-shaped drone but had evolved into an AI-powered pet raven. It hadn't been functioning quite right lately and was undergoing repairs and upgrades behind this very gate.

The guard opened the gate. A golf cart emerged.

"It's the twins." Pris exhaled loudly through glossy pink lips. "They'll fix this mess."

Geoffrey drove while Taylor studied a tablet, his glasses low on his nose. The golf cart pulled up to Pris's car, cop-car style. "Hey, Pris. We didn't know you were coming."

Pris shot a glance at Mickey. "Obviously. They won't let us in."

"Yeah, you aren't on the guest list. This isn't like Gemini; they are super strict here. Hang on." Gemini Robotics, a few miles away, belonged to Geoffrey and Taylor.

Mickey climbed out of the car and crossed to the golf cart. "Is this a big deal? I figured when you said, 'Do you want to come up for a couple of days' you meant 'you all,' meaning me and Pris. I know Mo is already here . . . " Mickey's voice trailed off.

Taylor swiped the tablet with his left hand. "Bao is coming."

"Should I just leave?" Pris clenched her jaw. "I mean, if you don't want me here. I know I'm not full-time science-y like you guys and Mo."

"It's not that. And you know programming."

"We don't even have our cameras," Mickey pointed out defensively. Usually, she and Pris brought their camera rigs everywhere. They never knew when something might come up that would make a good episode for the paranormal Contrary Crowcast. "You said not to bring them. This isn't even for the podcast."

"I came because Mickey thought we would have fun with your robots."

Geoffrey exchanged a glance with his twin. "Well, there will be some fun with robots."

The gates opened to let another cart through, driven by a man of Asian heritage, slightly older than Mickey and her friends, in his early thirties. Geoffrey and Taylor were half-Korean, but this man was a mixture of several ethnicities, giving his face sharp, handsome planes. He had a trim beard and glasses.

He pointed at Taylor. "What's going on?"

"Bao," Geoffrey explained, "Our friend Mickey arrived, the one we told you about. She brought our other friend, Pris. Can you authorize Pris on the guest list?" He turned to Mickey. "Mickey, this is Dr. Bao Lee, who is in charge of the medical aspects of Unieda Corporation."

Bao's glasses caught the light as he examined Mickey. She pressed her stump across her middle. He pointed his knuckle at her. "Your friend, you want her here? What's her name?"

"Yes? Pris Salamanca; she's my best friend. We do everything together." Why was this a big deal?

Bao wheeled his golf cart around to the security gate, spoke to the guard, and trundled back onto the campus, ignoring them.

After a minute, the guard leaned out and waved them through, handing the ID cards back to Pris. "You're all set," she said, her mouth clenched in a straight line.

The twins followed in their golf cart, and the gate closed behind them.

Pris left her car in a visitor space, and they hopped into the golf cart with their bags. The campus was so large it had overnight accommodations for guests and workers.

"That's the genetics workshop," Geoffrey pointed at one building, slightly off to the side of the largest, central building. All were clad in dark glass; the genetics building had another, even smaller building connected to it by a corridor. "Where Mo is working with Ananda for a little while, analyzing the mershark's DNA as part of Mo's program to get them to breed true with no need for either sharks or humans. It's going to make a great PhD thesis for her."

"This is where Ananda works?" Pris studied the campus, her pink buzz cut glinting in the golden fall sunlight.

Geoffrey continued, "Yes, and of course, she talks about us, and that got Bao interested in our work with the neural nets and Mind Meld." Ananda was the girlfriend of both twins. It worked for them. Mickey didn't ask for details.

"You're the queen of neural nets, Mickey, so Bao wants to meet you and see how you process information. And you'll get to play with our Mind Melds and maybe the cool new robots Unieda has been developing." Geoffrey drove through the parking lot and onto a paved path.

"Robo Rumble robots?" Pris perked up. One of the Mind Melds, Gemini's fighting robots, had won the International Robo Rumble Giant Golden Gear championship three times.

"No, more of a practical search-and-rescue robot." Taylor put down the tablet and pushed up his glasses, finally speaking. "They are very different from Mind Melds or any of the other traditional Robo Rumble robots."

Geoffrey parked the golf cart in a line of similar carts under a solar-panel roof. He plugged it in, and the four of them entered the robotics building.

-2-
Mickey

Smoked glass windows lined the ultramodern building's ground floor. Gray glass corridors connected matching buildings on either side. The buildings were crisp looking and soulless, the dark glass making them appear blind.

Bao waited just inside. He reached both hands to Mickey and then clasped them around her right hand, leaving her stump extended awkwardly. "I am so pleased to meet you. I only wish I might have met the wonderful surgeon who placed your neural implants, but Jeff and Tay tell me she has gone to the Great Beyond." The doctor was beaming the whole time he said this. "I have her notes, though, and now I have you."

Jeff and Tay? Mickey tried not to grimace. "Yes, here I am." She pulled her hand away. She hated being touched. "As requested."

Geoffrey moved to her side. "I reprogrammed the interface between your arm and the neural net. I also upgraded the software to the raven drone."

"Ek," Mickey corrected, naming the bird.

"Something already altered its software from the other two drones, even though it started out identical."

Mickey shrugged. She could guess why the raven had changed, but she didn't want to say anything in front of a stranger about how her enhanced mind influenced electronics.

Bao stared at Pris as the five of them walked along the outer corridor. "You look familiar. And you have the same name as that reality show family."

Pris tried to sidestep him, but he followed her.

Mickey elbowed Geoffrey. They all knew Pris hated talking about her famous family, and she refused to appear in their reality series.

Geoffrey said as a distraction, "What do you think of the altered programming on Mickey's raven drone, Pris? Any clue how it might have happened?"

Pris closed her eyes for a moment. "Changed in what way? Are you sure your brother didn't write it? Or someone else on your team?"

"Taylor's not much for programming. And it's not written correctly." He rubbed his cheek.

Pris had majored in computer science, where she had met the twins. "If it's not correct, how is it still working?"

"It's not that it's wrong." He paused. "There are proper formats, you know. Lines of code being indented a certain way, having explanatory comments. Best practices. None of that was followed. The code is all on top of itself and messy. It's tough to parse and understand."

"It works, though, right," Pris said.

Bao pointed at her. "It does." He squinted. "You really do look like—"

Mickey took his arm and grimaced at the contact. "What did you want from me?" She steered him away from her best friend and the tedious programming talk. They would start to discuss semicolon placement next, and her eyes would permanently roll back in her head from boredom. Imagine doing that for a living? Worrying about semicolons? Ugh.

The doctor's attention snapped to her. "*You* are a mystery I want to unravel." No one had ever looked at Mickey like that before. She had seen that sort of lustful leer in movies but never directed at her.

She didn't much like it, and she dropped her hand from his forearm. "A mystery?" She tried to laugh. "The only mysterious thing about me is how I got so injured as a newborn. I'm sure Taylor or Geoffrey told you that story."

Bao slowed, and Mickey did too, mindful of keeping him away from Pris. "They said your birth mother abandoned you."

"Someone abandoned me." There had been a time when Mickey had wondered who her birth mother had been. The supposition that the woman had been Native American was obvious, given Mickey's features and that someone had wrapped the newborn in a leather blanket with a toy crow made from real feathers. "My parents were doctors in the emergency department when first responders brought me in. My injuries were horrific." She raised her truncated arm and pointed at her deformed ribcage. "They didn't expect me to survive, and obviously, I had no insurance or family. My dad said they secretly called me Baby Jane Crow instead of Baby Jane Doe."

"What do they think happened to you?"

Mickey shrugged. "Car accident? They believe something crushed me somehow. My birth family couldn't afford the medical bills or didn't want to deal with an injured infant, so they left me at the fire station and hoped for the best."

"And your DNA profile says what?"

"Never had one. Don't want one. I'm easy to trace if my birth family wants to find me. My adoptive parents named me 'Crow.' I have a podcast with 'crow' in the title. I'm missing half an arm. I'm still in the area. My parents work at that same hospital. It's been over a quarter of a century. Obviously, they don't care."

Bao lifted his arm and tapped at the fancy smartwatch under his white lab coat. "That's an easy enough mystery to solve first thing. Then we can get on to the other tests." He pushed at a revolving door, leading Mickey into one of the glass tunnels.

"Tests? What tests?" Mickey followed him. They had lost her other friends somewhere along the way.

"Part of this week's agenda is to figure out why your neural net works so well and why you can do everything you can with it. Then, we will test its function on Tay's Mind Meld robots and my spidogs against some controls. We've got your refurbished arm for you, plus that bird drone. That drone is its own mystery."

"Tests?" Mickey repeated, a bit louder.

"Your buddy Melissa is here with Ana in the genetics lab. Apparently, you've met Ana?"

"Melissa? Oh, you mean Mo. Yes, I love Mo. And I've met Ananda a few times." She didn't know if Bao knew about the throuple thing. Some people got weird about relationships like that. "But I don't really want any tests."

These glass hallways must be punishingly hot in the summer and freezing in the winter. Mickey wondered aloud why they hadn't built tunnels instead.

"Unieda bought the campus buildings one at a time as other companies moved or went out of business. Eventually, we will dig tunnels," Bao explained, "But they aren't a priority. We own all the buildings now inside the security fence."

He used his smartwatch to activate the other revolving door and led Mickey into the genetics building.

She had never seen Mo professionally dressed in a lab coat with her braids pulled back in a headwrap before. Behind her usual rhinestone glasses, Mo's dark eyes appeared bigger. At least she was still wearing sneakers—this pair was red, and the beads and rings on her braids matched, even if those braids were subdued. The stretchy, wide material across her forehead was also red. Mo embraced Mickey gently; Mickey stroked her long, soft braids and stepped away, uncomfortable with human contact and being constrained.

Ananda fake-smiled at Mickey and gave a little finger wave. Her green nose stud matched her scrubs.

Equipment Mickey couldn't identify filled the laboratory room, along with things she recognized, like microscopes and test tubes, spread out on workbenches and carts. The spacious area gleamed with stainless steel like a high-tech kitchen, and most workers wore white lab coats over their scrubs.

Along one side of the space was a long, low fish tank divided into segments. Each segment contained weird lacy salamanders in many colors. Some were missing limbs and tails; others had extras. A few had bionic-looking replacements.

"Those are our experimental axolotls," Ananda explained. "They're Mexican salamanders. They regenerate and have other amazing properties. For instance, they easily accept artificial limbs, although we haven't figured out how to give them tiny neural nets yet."

Mickey didn't know whether to feel horrified or amazed that Ananda was giving tiny salamanders fake limbs. She headed straight for the tank. The axolotls all stared at her. They had adorable, smiling faces, even the deformed ones, seemingly very alert and aware. Without asking whether the creatures were venomous—or for permission—Mickey stuck her hand into the water. A black axolotl with a bifurcated tail crawled onto her fingers. She lifted it from the water, admiring its twin tails like that of a fancy goldfish. She held the creature to her face. They grinned at each other.

"Uh, Mickey—" Mo said.

Mickey turned, holding the black salamander next to

her cheek. It crept wetly from her hand onto her neck and explored the exposed connectors on the lower back part of her skull. Strangely, she didn't mind the axolotl touching her. "What?"

"You're handling an experimental animal."

The damp amphibian curled underneath her hair. "I'm not hurting it."

"Mickey, it's not a pet."

"It likes me."

Ananda sighed and marched over to Mickey, lifting her long dark hair and extracting the axolotl. It clutched the connectors, forcing her to pry it off Mickey. "It likes the attention. You can't play with it. It's destined for the scalpel."

"Obviously, it needs some play time before you murder it," Mickey snapped, appalled. "You're going to kill all of them?"

"Mickey, that's what lab animals are for," Mo explained. "Most of the time."

Mickey remembered the baby sharks Mo had set free, who had hated her even though Mo believed she had been kind to them.

Bao stepped forward, putting his hands on a lab bench. "We need to begin your tests now, Mickey."

Mickey couldn't help comparing herself to the axolotls. She tensed and backed away a few steps, right into Ananda, who had replaced the black salamander in the water. Another tech worked at the far end of the tank, tinkering with the filtration unit.

"Look," Ananda said. "We have your bird."

Bao pointed, and there was Ek, on a perch in the corner, deactivated. His red LED eyes were dark and unseeing, his body still.

"Allow us to take a little blood and a few pieces of skin, and we'll give you the neural net back, and then you can play with your drone." Bao's eyes were wide, his brows raised. "We need to run some tests on you with and without the neural net."

"Skin? Blood? I thought DNA tests were from spit." Mickey stared at Ek, dead in the corner.

"Those horrible commercial ones are. We do better ones, real ones," Ananda explained.

"I don't want to be tested, though." She took a few steps toward her raven.

Bao intercepted her and pointed at Ananda to stop her from crowding Mickey. "We did premium work upgrading and repairing that drone and the neural net. Your buddies over at Gemini might work for free, but they told us you would agree to some minor testing in exchange. We do government-grade military work here. I don't think you can afford to pay us."

Mickey turned her head. The damp spot where the axolotl had been curled on her neck felt cold. "You admit I am unique. So you should beg me for help. And you should be honored that you got to peek at my neural net at all and not be holding it hostage." She rubbed her face. Her hand smelled of axolotl—a bit swampy. "In fact, Pris and I recently found an awesome, huge fossil and some pre-Columbian artifacts and petroglyphs.* We're looking for a corporate sponsor for the dig and to pay for display space in a local museum." Mickey paused, letting the unspoken demand hang.

Mo hid her smile behind a handful of braids and opened a drawer, taking out the box holding Mickey's neural net. She cleaned the connections with an alcohol pad and glanced at Ananda with one eyebrow raised.

The technicians working in the lab had become distracted by this. Machines whirred unattended, pipettes dangled in lax hands, and no one peered through microscope eyepieces.

Mickey and Bao stared at each other, at an impasse. She widened her eyes.

He gave up first and pointed. "I was always going to fund your little fossil dig in exchange for a few tiny bone samples of the creature you found."

Mickey nodded once. She had expected nothing less.

Ananda lifted the small tablet that controlled Ek. "Before we do the testing with your neural net reattached, we want to see how your brain works without it. Come in here so Persephone can take a

---

*See the short story "Tusk" in the charity anthology *Something Woked This Way Comes* (https://amzn.to/4cUPmDS)

blood sample." Ananda led Mickey into a side room set up for phlebotomy.

Persephone, the phlebotomist, was so covered in a face mask, matching head cap, and scrubs that Mickey couldn't see anything but blue eyes and a bit of tanned skin. She ran a scanner over Mickey's tattooed right arm to locate the veins before inserting the needle and filling vial after vial of blood with different-colored stoppers.

Mickey felt queasy and uneasy. "You need that much for a DNA test?"

"I wouldn't know. I'm just doing what the paperwork says to take." Persephone's gloved hands expertly switched vials again, putting the filled ones into a rack. Mickey's blood appeared almost purple.

The edges of her vision darkened. "Can we maybe be done with this? I feel lightheaded. I think you're taking too much."

"Nonsense. I took twenty-eight vials from someone once, and they were just fine. I'll get you a cup of water in a moment."

Mickey closed her eyes, sensing the rigid, cold needle sucking blood from her inner elbow. When she first received her implants five years ago, she had been constantly aware of the embedded bits of metal in her stump and in her head. It had taken months to get used to them. It shouldn't bother her to have this extra tiny sliver of metal in her for a few minutes, but it did, reminding her of how it felt to have the xoggotli questing in her shoulder and neck and the shock when it had frozen and died, the shards of black glass falling out of her . . .

Persephone withdrew the needle, snapped the rubber cord off Mickey's biceps, and pressed a piece of gauze to the wound. "Hold this tight with your fingers—oh."

"Yeah," Mickey responded. "I can press it." She pushed her blunted forearm on the spot.

Persephone labeled the blood and retreated to get the promised water. Mickey counted sixteen tubes in the holder as she sipped lukewarm water. Persephone applied a few pieces of tape over the gauze to hold it in place.

In the main lab, Mickey reached for Ek's controller, but Ananda held it away. "First, we need to do all the scans while your brain is doing normal things."

Mickey felt her jaw set. "I don't really want to do any testing. I came here to help Geoffrey and Taylor with their robot."

"This is part of it." Ananda didn't hand over the tablet.

Mickey's inner elbow ached. "Can I have my prosthetic back first?"

"Not yet."

Bao took Mickey's truncated arm and led her across the laboratory, with Ananda and Mo following.

Mickey tried to pull her arm away. "You know, all through middle and high school, kids picked on me for being deformed and ugly and a freak. I was the plaything of all the mean girls. They would take my art supplies and break them or hide them. Tear up my drawings. Make fun of me. They could never just leave me alone to do what I wanted. That's exactly how I am feeling today."

"No." Bao was practically dragging her. "I think you are wonderful. I've been so eager to meet you. And for you to meet my spidogs."

Mickey duly allowed a cheerful middle-aged woman everyone called Aunt Lagatha to x-ray her head, chest, and left forearm in a dozen different ways. Aunt Lagatha looked like a Valkyrie, with long silver-and-gold braids down her back, and she towered over Bao.

Aunt Lagatha was grateful to have a human patient for once and that she did not have to forcibly sedate Mickey.

Mickey wondered how much force and sedation a tiny delicate axolotl required and decided she didn't want to know.

Aunt Lagatha laid Mickey on a table that slid in and out of a noisy machine, and immobilized her neck in a cradle. She took images of Mickey's head while Mickey thought about why there were chain-mail gloves and aprons hanging on the wall.

Aunt Lagatha carefully removed skin scrapings from both of Mickey's arms in places that wouldn't ruin her tattoos, depositing the cells in test tubes and on slides.

Mickey wondered what her parents would think about all these tests. "Hey, can I get copies of all my test results? My parents are doctors."

"These are all classified, honey," Aunt Lagatha explained. "We do government and DOD work here. Bao, didn't you have her sign the paperwork?"

"The inside of my own head is classified to me?"

Bao pointed. Mickey really wanted to snap off his finger. "Ana, honey, can you have your friend sign all the nondisclosure paperwork?"

She's not my friend, Mickey thought. She wasn't sure she even liked Ananda. But she also thought Bao should not call Ananda "honey" in a business situation.

The tablet Ananda handed her had a lot of hard-to-read small print and legalese about how Mickey couldn't talk to anyone about anything she saw here on this classified visit. It also permitted Unieda to use Mickey's test results and samples for whatever they wanted, with no compensation to or recognition of Mickey.

"What if I don't sign this? Do you give me my arm and neural net and my raven, throw away my blood, and allow me and Pris to go home?" And where was Pris?

Bao shook his head. "These samples pay for the alterations to the tech. We agreed to throw in the fossil dig and museum exhibit as a completion bonus. And you don't own any of the tech; Tay and Jeff do."

A shock shook Mickey. "Since when?"

Ananda smirked a little. Her smooth brown face morphed instantly from pretty girl to mean girl. Mickey was sure now that they weren't friends. "Since always."

Mo stepped forward. Mickey had forgotten she was there. "Of course, you own your own tech." She glared at Ananda. "We will iron this out. Take Ek for a little fly here, and then go next door and meet the new robots while we start on your blood tests."

Ananda's cheeks pinkened.

Mo held out her hand. Ananda handed over the tablet that controlled Ek. Mo immediately gave it to Mickey.

Mickey clicked it on and connected to the raven. It moved slowly, an animal awakening from a long sleep, stretching its massive black wings, moving each leg, cocking its neck. Finally, Ek opened its eyes. They had always been bright red LEDs but now they were dulled, almost black.

The connection to Ek felt muted without her neural net. Mickey wasn't able to see properly through its eyes. Everything was flat and the colors looked off. There was no sound or proprioception. She had to rely on the tablet, which she hated. The neck strap had gone missing, so she had trouble holding it and using it simultaneously with only one hand.

Ek cawed and lifted from the makeshift perch. Although it flew like a bird, close-up, the whirr of its battery-powered motors was audible. It landed with a thump on Mickey's left shoulder and rubbed its beak on her ear.

A blond technician, name badge "Doug," came forward and peered at the tablet. "Where are those commands? I thought I put that drone through everything it could do."

"It's not your raven," Mickey said. "Do you even know its name?"

Doug blinked. "The drone has a name?"

Exactly.

Bao held both forefingers before his lips. "You haven't even got the neural net on."

"No. I'm not connected very well. And if you won't give me back my arm, I'll need the missing strap for the tablet."

Another round in Aunt Lagatha's machine while she tried to see through Ek's eyes and control it from the other room with the tablet. The raven sat on the edge of the extended axolotl tank, where the black salamander with the beautiful bifurcated tail swam leisurely up to it. The wicked, long beak touched the soft, smiling face gently.

As the table jerked and whirred, Mickey thought for a second she connected to the black axolotl.

-3-
Mickey

In the robotics lab, Pris and Geoffrey sat at a corner desk with three curved computer screens, staring at what Mickey assumed was computer code. Geoffrey waved his arms while Pris's head was tilted, one eye squinting.

This room was several stories tall, industrial and dark gray, looking unfinished. Machine-shop tools and workbenches lined three walls, littered with metal and electronic components, interspersed with a few doors. In the center of the room were pallets of materials. The final wall was glass, looking into another cavernous unfinished room.

Taylor sat on the floor in between two hulking, almost identical robots. His glasses were falling off his nose. He had a pair of wire cutters in his mouth as he peered into one robot's exposed innards.

"You know the Mind Meld robots," Bao pointed.

Mickey nodded. "I was there in college when they were being invented. They were much smaller back then. And there was only one."

The Mind Melds had tank treads on the bottom of stubby legs, lifting arms like bulldozer blades, and they spit flames. The twins operated them via a less sophisticated neural net than Mickey's (requiring no implant), a remote-control box and virtual reality goggles, or a combination of the two.

A few yards away, three other robots crouched. These were very different in design from the Mind Melds. White instead of black, sleek, curved, long-legged, like a monstrous hybrid of dogs and spiders, very heavy on the spider. No one worked on them. They just waited.

"These are my spidogs," Bao said. "We have three prototypes ready to test." They had bands of color painted around their many ankles—yellow, blue, and red. Yellow had a number 1 on its sleek rounded back, Blue number 2, and Red number 3. "SPIDOG stands for 'Synthetic Proprioceptive Intelligence Defense-Offense Ground Scout,' but they are just spider-dogs, or spidogs. They have three different modes of programming: search-and-rescue dog, which we'll be testing this week, war dog, and guard dog. We think the spider form is an improvement on other companies' dog form."

The Mind Melds looked like what they were: massive pieces of metal designed to smash into and destroy other gigantic pieces of metal, loudly and in the most destructive way possible. Combat robots, fighting robots. The Mind Melds were honest.

The spidogs were sneaky, creepy, and smooth. Mickey thought that if a robot could lie to you, the spidogs would lie. If she was trapped under a building, she would not trust one of these spidogs to find and save her.

Ek leaped from her shoulder and landed on Yellow, attempting to poke its beak between the spaces of its white armor.

"Your drone is lucky that they are powered down and only in search mode. Otherwise, it would be a pile of feathers and components on the floor," Bao remarked.

Taylor pulled an earplug from his ear and waved at Mickey, the tool still clamped between his lips. Tinny music pulsed from between his fingers, and then he wiggled it back into his ear.

Ek continued to prod at Yellow as if searching for a worm inside its armor. Mickey, still hazy with the poor connection, thumbed at the controller screen.

Yellow whirred. Its many limbs unfolded. Standing on six legs, it looked even more like a spider. It kept its two front legs held up like praying mantis forearms. The mouthparts of its head gnashed. The yellow-white LEDs of its many eyes blinked.

"It's not supposed to do that," Bao said. He raised his voice. "Taylor?"

Ek hopped onto Red as Yellow turned all its eyes onto the black feathered drone.

Taylor finally pulled out his earphones and raised his eyebrows.

"Yellow!" Bao shouted. "It's awake!"

Ek attempted to remove a piece of curved white armor from Red's dormant head. Mickey had no control over the raven anymore.

Something clattered in the corner where Geoffrey and Pris had been sitting, and a pair of raised voices carried. "Yellow?" Geoffrey yelled.

"Yellow!" Bao replied.

The cluster of eye lights on Yellow's head blinked out. Yellow sank back into a resting pose just as Red's constellation of crimson eyes lit.

"Red!" Bao added. "Now Red is up!"

Red was just unfolding its many legs and joints when its lights went out. It ungracefully collapsed.

"Blue?" Geoffrey called.

Mickey, Bao, and Ek stared at the third spidog. It stayed quiescent.

"Sleeping still!"

Taylor, cross-legged on the floor, held the wire cutters up like a knife. He glanced at his fist and laughed. "I don't know what I thought I was going to do. Rewire it on the fly?"

Ek retreated to Mickey's shoulder. If the raven was chastised by what had just happened, she couldn't tell.

"That was exciting." Mickey took a few steps away from Bao and his spidogs.

Pris, panting and laughing, came around a pallet with Geoffrey. "What just happened? We were trying to dissect this insane code, and then all you guys started yelling."

Mickey gave a one-shoulder shrug. "Two of the spider-dogs woke up spontaneously when Ek landed on them. Perhaps they don't like other robots."

"That shouldn't matter," Taylor said. "They work in teams. They don't like or dislike other robots. There is no code for that."

"At least they were still plugged into the network, so we could finish tweaking their programming." Geoffrey poked at Red, who didn't respond, and explained to Mickey, "They have a fail-safe that keeps hackers out. When they are in war dog or patrol dog mode, we don't want anyone to be able to hack in and shut them down. You must physically connect to it."

Red's viciously sharp mandibles stayed curled, and its eyes remained dark. Mickey did not like the spidogs at all.

-4-
Mickey

Doug, the one who claimed to be able to operate Ek, brought a clear plexiglass box perforated with holes into the warehouse-sized room on the other side of the glass from where they gathered with the five robots. A big two-toned rat sat inside the box, looking around.

Mickey wanted to save that rat.

"Emilio!" Bao called. "Do you want to operate Blue?"

A little, mustached man emerged from one of the side doors. Mickey's first thought was to wonder if Emilio was literally going to ride the spidog. He was barely taller than the robot.

"What're we doing, boss?" Emilio asked.

"Search and rescue of a rat."

Emilio turned his back to the wall of windows.

Doug placed the rat's box inside a wooden crate piled with other wooden crates. He flashed a thumbs-up to the windows and left the arena area.

Another white-coated technician unhooked Blue from a cable Mickey hadn't noticed. Emilio pulled a pair of what appeared to be blue VR goggles over his large forehead and lifted a matching controller from a nearby workbench.

Blue's LED eyes were, predictably, incandescently azure. The cluster lit first, and then Blue's legs unfolded. The pointed tips of each leg expanded into gripping toes with deadly points. The robot was over three feet tall when standing. Blue's mouthparts clicked together as if it was eager to go.

Someone opened the large door, and Blue tip-tapped into the arena on spiked toes.

Emilio stood at the window on a stepstool, both hands operating the controller. His head swiveled as the goggles followed the robot. It stalked through the piles of boxes.

Bao explained, "Blue can sense the heat and heartbeat from the rat. Usually, no one would do a search and rescue for anything that tiny. Nothing smaller than an infant, maybe ten to fifteen pounds, something the size of a cat or small dog. But if our spidogs can consistently find something as tiny as a rat, finding a human child or adult will be easy for them. We change up the configuration of what's in the arena between each test as well."

Emilio had not seen where Doug had hidden the rat. Now Mickey understood why the little man had turned his back. Blue approached each obstacle and circled it. Although its body configuration was arachnoid, it acted more like a dog. It appeared to be sniffing at the piles. A few times, it used one of the front arm-legs to move a box aside and inspect a different box. Blue was nowhere near the rat yet.

Mickey asked Bao, "What does Emilio control and what does the spidog do on its own?"

"The spidogs walk on their own. They process heat signatures and can sense vital life signs like heartbeats, although the operator can see that as well. They have their own sense of balance. There's a speaker inside it so the operator can communicate with any people any people in its vicinity and give instructions or warnings. Someday, they will be completely autonomous, but for now, they still need some human guidance on which direction to go, where to search next, and when to give up. But the limited AI inside each spidog gets better with every iteration."

Pris stood beside Mickey and elbowed her. "This is crazy. With those goggles, Emilio can see through the spidog's eyes. It's also being recorded."

Mickey squinted at her, knowing how Pris thought. "We have enough cameras. And we have Ek back again. The Contrary Crowcast doesn't need a war dog."

"It's cool, though."

"Ek is cooler and way less scary."

"Blue isn't scary."

Mickey raised her eyebrows. Inside the arena, a pile of cardboard cartons crashed to the concrete floor. Mickey winced and glanced away. "Is the rat okay?"

"Nowhere near the rat yet," Pris assured her.

Taylor and Geoffrey were having their own intense conversation while watching the spidog work, but Mickey couldn't hear them. Bao stood next to Emilio, giving him instructions and probably messing up the test.

Blue snapped to alertness. Its mouth pinchers clattered, audible even through the glass. The spidog was crouched near where Doug had hidden the rat. Had Bao told Emilio where it was, or had the robot actually sensed the tiny rodent through layers of acrylic and wood?

Blue used its arm-legs to pull away each crate and inspect it. The rat was in the center of a pile. As the robot got closer to the acrylic box, its movements slowed and became more precise. It broke up the wooden boxes and poked inside with its jittering mouth pieces, searching for the rat.

If Mickey had been the rat, she would not want to be found by this thing.

Blue located the correct box and extracted the plexiglass cage, holding it with its arm-legs and studying the rat. The rat must have gone through this exercise before because it appeared bored, not terrified. It rubbed its pink paws over its black head. Blue sniffed all along one side of the box and then inserted the sharp tip of one mandible into a breathing hole and started to rip the plastic box open.

"Stop it!" Bao called.

Emilio manipulated the controller until the fangs withdrew. Blue cradled the cracked box to its carapace and headed back to the door where it waited, bouncing slightly, to be let back into the robot lab with its prize.

Doug gave the rat a biscuit and took it away.

Emilio powered down Blue.

Bao turned to Mickey. "Could you operate that robot?"

Mickey shook her head and clicked her tongue. "Nope."

Bao's mouth turned down inside his precise beard, and he glared at Geoffrey with narrowed eyes.

Geoffrey shrugged and turned his hands up.

"I haven't got two hands," Mickey continued. "Emilio used both hands to hold and manipulate the controller. I can't do that, obviously. I can't even get you to give me my prosthetic back."

"If we modified the controls so you could operate it with your neural net. That's what I meant." Bao backpedaled.

"Maybe?" She didn't like the spidogs, and she didn't want to play with them. She could visit the Mind Melds at Gemini anytime. She just wanted to go home.

"How about you, Priscilla? Could you use that controller?"

"My name is Pris, Dr. Lee, and I could absolutely use that controller."

"Call me Bao."

"Yes, Dr. Lee."

Mickey understood. When nearly everyone around had a doctorate, calling people "Doctor" seemed silly, and thus, using first names was preferable. But Bao seemed determined to misname everyone he met. She wondered if Aunt Lagatha even enjoyed being called that. She could prefer to be called Laggie.

"It will take a little while for you to convert one of the spidogs to neural control. Why don't we come back another day? Pris and I will send you the information about the fossil dig."

Taylor chewed his lip. "Actually, Mickey, we've been working on that part for a while. This invitation wasn't spontaneous."

Mickey pushed her face to one side. On her shoulder, Ek ruffled its wings. She had forgotten how much it weighed and how comforting that weight was.

Bao lifted his wrist and pushed back his white sleeve to look at his smartwatch. His eyebrows met. "Mickey, they have your DNA results, and Ana wants to see you in the lab about them."

"We should have made a betting pool for which tribe she is," Pris said to Taylor.

"You're assuming she's Native. She could be Asian," Geoffrey argued.

"She is standing right here," Mickey said.

-5-
Mickey

On the other side of the tunnel, Mickey and Bao, with Pris trailing them, settled in a conference room with Mo, Ananda, and Aunt Lagatha.

Ek fluttered from Mickey's shoulder and started exploring the side table, knocking over an empty glass.

Mickey rolled her eyes. "Let me guess, I'm Pocahontas's great-times-a-hundred granddaughter and also Sitting Bull's?"

Aunt Lagatha folded her hands before her face with her elbows on the table. "Exactly the opposite."

"I'm a time traveler, and Pocahontas is my granddaughter? No, wait, I am Pocahontas?" She inspected her tattoos and missing arm. "The historical record seems inaccurate."

Mo snorted and tried to hide her face behind her sleek braids.

"You aren't related to Pocahontas at all. That's not how it works. We would need to have a sample of her actual DNA—although she does have living descendants. Based on what we can determine, though, we are absolutely certain you are not related to her."

"That doesn't make any sense." Pris said what Mickey was thinking. "You are saying you can prove a negative."

Aunt Lagatha closed her eyes and leaned her face against her folded hands. She was much older than everyone else at the table. The silver streaks in her golden hair and the shallow wrinkles on her face gave her a tired appearance. "I know a lot about medicine. Mickey's brain scans were quite odd but still in the realm of human variation, statistically. There's a continuum of what's considered 'normal' for everything, and you're teetering on the far edge," she said to Mickey. "It's enough to make a note of, surely. Not enough to write a paper about."

Mickey nodded. People were weird. As much as Geoffrey and Taylor looked identical, except for Taylor's glasses, they were mirror twins, something rare that Ananda had discovered when they enrolled in her twins study for her PhD. Taylor had *situs inversus*—he wasn't just left-handed as opposed to Geoffrey being right-handed; his organs were all in the opposite places, too. Whatever weirdness was in her brain was probably just as rare but not unheard of. Plus, after five years of implants, her brain might be functioning a bit differently than other people's brains now.

The older woman continued. "I didn't even mention those findings to you after the first set of scans, or the second, because I didn't think they were significant, or at least not yet. But then Ananda and Mo worked on sequencing your DNA. We have the fastest equipment here—it takes hours, not weeks, to get results. The results are more precise than if you spit in a tube and mailed it off after paying eighty bucks on sale for a list of your supposed relatives."

"So, Pocahontas is not on my list of relatives. Everyone around me says I'm Native American, not me."

Mo rubbed a braid on her lips and stared at Pris, her eyes big and worried.

"It's just that—" Aunt Lagatha paused. "No one is your relative, dear. Ana ran the test twice. You aren't related to anyone in any DNA database. And we have access to all of them."

Mickey cocked her head. "I don't understand."

"We don't either. If we look back enough generations, everyone is related to everyone else. Except you. Your particular mitochondrial DNA doesn't appear anywhere else. And there is mtDNA going back to before humans were, well, human. But you don't appear to be part of any of those lineages. There are haplogroups showing human migration going back to someone we call Mitochondrial Eve in Africa, and every person eventually traces back to her, 170,000 years ago, but somehow your DNA doesn't match up with any haplogroup in our database."

Mickey turned over her hand and stared at the lines there. "I'm not human?"

"You are totally human, Mickey, of course," Mo said fiercely, dropping her braids. The beads clinked.

"Just maybe not from here," Aunt Lagatha finished, clenching her folded hands into a fist. *Here?* What did *here* mean? "We have nothing more to go on. This makes no sense—"

"You have more to go on, though." Pris leaned forward. "Right, Mickey?"

Mickey frowned at her best friend.

Pris's pale cheeks were pink with excitement. "The crow bundle, right."

Mickey tilted her head.

"The crow and the blanket. Don't your parents have them?"

Mickey's lips parted. "Yeah. They do. My dad had them sealed in some kind of archive box, and he has the box locked up somewhere."

"What's the crow bundle?" Bao demanded, leaning forward, beard quivering.

Mickey explained, again, the leather blanket and the crow toy left with the broken baby at the fire station.

"They came with you when your birth parents abandoned you?"

Mickey nodded. "I wasn't there. I mean, I was there, but I was barely born so I don't remember. Only what my parents say. A crushed newborn, wrapped up with this toy. The hospital saved everything in case my birth parents ever claimed me, but no one did. When my parents adopted me, my dad took the bag with my possessions and had it preserved. It's nasty; the leather blanket is all stained with blood."

Bao's eyes widened. "Would your parents allow us access to the bundle, do you think?"

"Mickey, this is probably exactly the reason he saved it," Mo said. "He's a medical doctor. DNA testing was just starting to be a thing back then."

"I'll drive back down and grab it," Pris volunteered.

Mickey texted her parents. Today, they were both working, but she didn't remember their hours. Her dad was available soon. She arranged for Pris to pick up the archival box—he was even willing to drive to a rest stop partway and meet her.

She didn't tell her dad she wasn't truly human.

Or that she was possibly an alien.

-6-
Mickey

While Taylor helped to figure out why Yellow and Red had malfunctioned, Geoffrey headed to the DNA lab to give Mickey her prosthetic arm and neural net back.

The neural net was a shining diadem of wires and magnets, a science-fiction crown instead of a fantasy one. It snapped onto the back of Mickey's head just above her neck. She pushed it in place under her long, dark hair and shifted it until the magnets caught the connectors in her skull. It was all very cyberpunk.

Her world immediately got bigger, so much so that Mickey swayed in place and almost fell. She hadn't realized how small she had felt these past weeks, how unconnected to the world she was.

Everyone else lived like that their whole lives.

Ek stirred on her shoulder, stretched his neck and wings, and eyed her. She saw herself through the drone's eyes, a skinny young woman who was probably some kind of Native American no matter what their stupid DNA tests said, metal shining from the back of her head through her hair.

Doug murmured, "She isn't even touching the controller. How is she getting that drone to do those things?"

Geoffrey laid her prosthetic arm on the table. Mickey inserted her forearm stump, rotating it until the embedded rare-earth magnetic contacts clicked to hold it in place. She flexed the metal fingers and smiled as he strapped the metal and leather device to her elbow and upper arm. She still didn't have full dexterity, but it was better than any off-the-shelf, flesh-colored replacement her parents had ever gotten her. And it was strong, as strong as the straps and magnets could make it.

Bao leaned over. "How do you control the fingers?"

Mickey held up the black metal hand. "How do you control your fingers?" She wiggled those fingers at him. "I just think about it, and they move."

"Are you using the neural net or your nerves?"

"Yes," Mickey replied.

"Can we do some tests?"

Mickey slow-blinked at him, and it wasn't in the affectionate way of a cat. "I'm not picking up eggs for you. Or putting rods in holes. Anything like that. I did all that a hundred times when I got the arm. It's all on video."

Bao frowned.

Geoffrey's smartwatch beeped at him, and he left the room.

Mickey and Ek walked over to the long tank. The black bifurcated-tail axolotl swam to meet them. It seemed to have no fear about climbing onto her metal left hand.

"Mickey," Mo warned. "Don't get attached."

"Why does it have two tails?"

The salamander explored the prosthetic.

"I cut its tail off," Ananda explained. "Then I put experimental growth hormone on the wound, and two tails grew back."

The frilly axolotl appeared plumper and larger than Mickey remembered, and its beautiful tails seemed to be longer, although the amphibian didn't look as pretty outside of the water. She touched its head, petting it. Above and between its eyes, a shiny bump caught the light like a gemstone. Had it resulted from another of Ananda's experiments? As the axolotl skittered onto Mickey's tattoo, it glanced up, grinning, and she definitely connected with it for a moment. It saw her as somehow like itself.

"You have so many," Mickey said to Ananda. "Would you miss this one?"

"Mickey, if you want an axolotl, I can help you design a nice enclosure and get you one—even a black one. But not this black one." Mo plucked the little guy off Mickey's arm and returned it to its tank.

The black axolotl with two tails hung at the tank's edge, staring at Mickey while the others around it went about their amphibious business, their feathery gills waving.

"We need to do another round of testing." Bao pointed at Mickey, ignoring the tension in the room.

"You're an old hand at this now," Aunt Lagatha said. "It will be as quick as I can make it."

Mickey made certain Ek held tightly to her shoulder and connected to the axolotl. It understood that everyone there were people, but she seemed to have a unique aura that made the little amphibian long for her. She withdrew and wondered how long it could live outside of water and how quickly Mo could set up a tank.

Ek stirred and whirred as she regained light control of the drone. His programming *was* different. If Mickey hadn't been told, she would have just assumed the twins had upgraded the drone yet again, giving it more advanced AI capabilities.

If they hadn't reprogrammed Ek, who had? Had he really just evolved from being in contact with her mind?

Ek launched onto a workbench in the main room as Mickey sat on the moving, scanning table in the side office. Her artificial hand rubbed the scar on her neck where the glass shards had emerged after the xoggotli creature had died trying to infiltrate her brain.

Ananda had made a careless mistake that day, and they had salvaged none of the xoggotli glass from the ground or under the water beside Fright Island Theme Park. But all these scans today had shown no glass-like shards still in her neck. There was no reason for the sharp, pricking sensations Mickey still felt there.

Aunt Lagatha positioned Mickey on the table while Bao waved his forefinger around. "You're connected to the drone, right?"

"Yes."

"What can you make it do?"

"Whatever a bird can do and more."

"Even though it's in the other room?"

"Yes." Mickey remembered controlling three of the bird drones at once while they were all out of her sight, frantically trying to save Pearl, Starfish, and the rest of the mersharks from being blown up. Just hooking into Ek on the other side of a wall was nothing.

The bed moved forward and backward, scanning her head, as she and Ek dive-bombed the lab workers and inspected the equipment. Doug watched everything the raven did, mouth hanging open. Obviously, he had made the mistake of thinking Ek was just a fancy-looking drone. Ek landed on Doug's shoulder, headbutted him in the jaw, and winked at him. Mickey wanted to laugh, but she was supposed to stay still while the machine read her mind. She could almost read Doug's mind. Doug and the controller could accomplish none of what she could get Ek to do, not in weeks or months of trying. Mickey and Ek had a special bond; that was why Geoffrey and Taylor had given her the raven.

Finally, the table slid all the way out of the machine, freeing Mickey. Bao helped her off the thin foam pad. She really didn't need assistance, but the table was uncomfortable, and she was glad to be off it.

"I'm going to study these and compare them to the earlier tests," Aunt Lagatha said. "I'll send them over to some other radiologists to see what they think if I find anything interesting."

Although Mickey gazed longingly at the black bifurcated axolotl, Bao dragged her past the tank and out through the revolving doors. At least he was holding her prosthetic and not her flesh.

"Do you guys eat lunch?" She complained. "Can I take a few minutes to shove a protein bar and a bottle of water into my face?"

Bao glanced at his smartwatch. Mickey hadn't seen him use a phone once. Just how smart was that watch? Pris would soon be researching where to buy super-smart watches. Pris bought her clothes at secondhand stores and her tech the minute it came out.

"It is lunchtime, isn't it? We have a building with a cafeteria, and then we can see how you use the spidogs."

After a meal of delicious chicken nuggets with exquisite hot sauce, Mickey returned to the robotics lab, where the three spidogs remained asleep. She adjusted the neural net on the back of her head, not used to having it again, and stared at the crouched metal figures. She still didn't like them.

Geoffrey barely touched her shoulder. "We have training pieces for you to practice on. Spare legs and eyes."

Mickey turned gratefully from the menacing trio and followed her friend to a corner where someone had laid out spare spidog limbs and even a head on a workbench, all connected by thin wires to a power supply.

She flew Ek onto a nearby shelf and left him there under his own power. She stepped closer to the bench and touched a leg with her flesh hand and then with her prosthetic hand. The limb was inert. Lifeless. She reached out with the part of her mind that connected to electronics and let it float around. The room was heavy with things begging for her attention. She picked out the biggest ones, the spidogs and the Mind Melds. Some others opened to her, and she turned to Geoffrey.

"You have serious cyber security holes here. Anyone could tap into this stuff like I'm doing. Tell Taylor."

"I don't think just anyone could do it, Mickey; that's the whole point of you being here. Because only you can do this."

She made a sideways face and narrowed down the connections until she found the leg under her fingers.

It twitched.

Mickey lifted away her hands and tilted her head. The foot spikes expanded from the leg's base. She pushed it, and it balanced upright. Mickey activated the other spare legs and stood them all on their spiked toes. She entered the head nub and turned on the orange LED eyes. The world, seen through them, was not tinted orange, but it was fractured and strange. The software correctly identified everyone in its visual range as people, but the rest of the programming seemed lacking. Although Ek was in its sight and moving, Orange did not target or identify the drone.

"That's a problem," Mickey remarked. "I know Ek looks like a bird and acts like one, but he has the heat signature of the drone that he is, and the head isn't even noticing him when he's in direct line of sight."

"That's strange." Geoffrey bent to peer into the orange eyes.

Mickey recoiled at the way his face appeared through the grouping of orange LED eyes. "Don't do that. It's too weird."

The legs on the bench hopped. One toppled over, and Mickey stood it back up. They tapped their wickedly pointed toes and flexed them. It wasn't much different from how she moved her fingers. Making the individual legs hop all together was harder because they weren't attached to a body, and she had to balance them while they hopped.

Emilio emerged from his office-slash-closet and stood too close to Mickey, watching the animated legs. "You're doing that with the thing on your head?"

She nodded. "And the things in my head." She inched away.

"Yo, Geoffrey, you gonna teach me to do this?"

"We would have to drill holes in your skull first," Bao said.

"Can I see?" Emilio actually reached up for Mickey's hair.

The legs crashed down, twitching. Mickey stepped away and held up her hands. "Please don't touch me."

"Okay, I just wanna look." Emilio pressed his lips together, but he didn't sound sorry.

"My neural net has been getting repaired here for weeks. Don't tell me you never studied it."

"I looked at it, but I didn't understand what you'd be able to do. It wasn't connected or on your head."

"It's the same, but on my head." Mickey stood the legs back on their pointed feet. The toes kicked. The orange eye lights flickered in the same pattern. If she knew Morse code, it would have said, "Keep away." Or "Go away." She hated having people crowd her and touch her. Unieda was proving to be a very touchy-feely bunch, and Mickey was unhappy.

Bao watched everything she did, blinking rapidly and occasionally speaking into his watch or waving his finger around. "You think you could run a whole spidog?"

Mickey shrugged. "I don't know the protocols for their search-and-rescue stuff or any of the war dog or guard dog functions. Could I make it move and search for a rat in a box in a maze? I think so."

He started to ask something else, and then his smartwatch buzzed. Bao glanced at it. "Your friend is back with those items from when you were a baby."

-7-
Mickey

Mickey couldn't remember the last time she had seen her crow and blanket. Her parents had preserved them, true, but Aunt Lagatha treated the package as if it held precious ancient artifacts. Even Mickey couldn't enter the clean room.

"Especially you," Aunt Lagatha told her. "We can't have you contaminating your own samples."

Mickey stood between Pris and Mo at the observation window. Ananda stayed back with the other lab workers. Aunt Lagatha didn't allow Bao into the clean room, either. Aunt Lagatha suited up until she looked like a marshmallow in the airlock. Air and liquid showers decontaminated her, and only then did she pass into the clean room with Mickey's crow bundle.

Mickey's adoptive dad had wrapped her infant artifacts in layers of clean brown paper inside a special archival bag. Remote-controlled cameras documented Aunt Lagatha opening the bag and unwrapping the crinkly paper on top of a stainless-steel table.

The small, beaded leather blanket had perhaps once been soft, but now it appeared stiff in Aunt Lagatha's blue-gloved hands. Some of the tiny edging beads were missing. Others fell off onto the table as the old, brittle thread snapped.

"I think it used to be almost white," Mickey whispered, feeling silly for speaking in a hush. It was her blanket, her toy, not some artifacts belonging to Baby Jesus. But now that these things were revealed, she wanted to run in there and grab them. *Mine! Don't touch!* Out of sight for her really had been out of mind all these years. Now she stared with everyone else at what Aunt Lagatha was exposing.

The once-soft pale suede was cracked, stained, brown, and stiff. Aunt Lagatha snapped photos as she tried to lay it flat on the table. It curled up after over twenty years of being tightly folded. Flakes of what was probably blood joined the beads on the stainless-steel table.

"Some of that blood might be your birth mother's," Mo mused. "If you were injured that badly so close to birth, chances are she was right there with you, of course, and perhaps was also hurt."

Left unspoken was the question of whether or not Mickey's birth mother had survived whatever trauma had disfigured her just-born daughter so badly.

Aunt Lagatha left the blanket curled on itself like a dead spider on its back, picked up the other, smaller package, and started the slow, careful process of unwrapping it.

The stuffed crow was in sad shape. It appeared to be made of similar leather as the blanket, dyed black, with small black feathers sewn on and black beads for eyes. Some feathers were broken or missing. One feather fluttered to the floor as Aunt Lagatha inspected the small toy.

It was just the right size for an infant to clutch.

"Terribly unhygienic," Bao remarked. "Giving a newborn baby nasty feathers to play with."

"Some people are terribly poor," Pris, who was unimaginably wealthy, said. "Mickey's birth mom loved her enough to give her something to hug, even if it's not up to your standards."

"Those are real feathers. They will have bird DNA. That leather will have DNA, too. And all that blood." Mo leaned forward to watch as Aunt Lagatha took samples and documented where each came from. "She has to cut the leather up a little and take a feather."

"Yeah," Mickey agreed to the desecration. "I haven't seen that stuff in years. It's okay. I'm not attached. If my parents were willing to give Pris the bundle and they know what's going on, it's okay with them. I wouldn't even have any of it if they hadn't saved it from the hospital. I wouldn't even know about it." Even so, as she watched Aunt Lagatha take careful samples, she winced.

"Baby Jane Crow," Pris said with a smile.

Mo smiled, too. "Baby Jane something. We will figure it out. There is no way you aren't related to anyone. If your mother's blood is on there, that will help."

"Surely I'm related to my birth mother."

"Of course," Mo answered. "And she's got to be related to someone else."

"You would think," Pris said. "Right?"

Aunt Lagatha wrapped Mickey's items up in Unieda-approved archival materials and exited the clean room with all the samples.

"Looks like I have to go back to work," Mo said, "finding all of Mickey's secrets." Swinging her braids beneath her red headwrap, she walked over to a lab bench to receive a sealed sample container from Aunt Lagatha.

Bao pointed at Pris. "Do you want to learn how to operate a spidog robot? I could use an inexperienced control to go against Mickey's neural net and my own expert driver."

"I don't know how to control robots. I've used the bird drones, right, but this seems bigger. And I thought we were here for Taylor and Geoffrey and the Mind Melds."

"You are going to go up against them." Bao waved his finger.

"Like, a mini Robo Rumble event right here? Mind Meld versus spidog? Because those spidogs are delicate and wimpy. Either Mind Meld will trash them." Pris avoided the pointing finger.

"Don't believe what you think you see, and no, the robots won't fight each other. This is going to have more finesse, be more of a proof of concept."

"The only concept Mind Meld has is to crush other robots," Pris said. "Mickey and I have known Taylor and Geoffrey since college when Mind Meld only weighed fifty pounds and Mickey's naked brain had zero implants. Mind Meld doesn't finesse, right."

"Right, Priscilla," Bao said. "We currently have these three spidogs working on search and rescue. The future goal is to turn them loose in a disaster area and allow them to work independently to find and extract victims. Right now, their human operator guides them much more than their programming."

"Right." Pris seemed unconvinced, biting her pink-glossed lip.

"You and Mickey will be two of their three operators today. But what if the disaster area also had hostiles in it? A war zone, maybe? We haven't figured out how to incorporate all three functions of the spidogs into one package. So, if they are working as soldiers, war dogs, they will not rescue someone. If they are rescuing people, they won't fight. We need to see how far we can push them. While they are 'rescuing' the rats tomorrow, the two Mind Melds will be actively trying to thwart them."

"Taylor and Geoffrey will be operating their Mind Melds?" Pris asked.

Bao nodded. "This could be valuable intel. Out in the field, we might need a totally inexperienced person to pick up the controls of a spidog. That would be you, Pris. Then we have the very experienced operator, Emilio. Then we have our dream operator in Mickey, not fully trained but intuitive and able to connect in ways no one else can. We will see how the different spidogs react to being harried by the Mind Melds, and then we can tweak their programming or physical structure as needed."

They started across the glass corridor between buildings. "Why can't you just put all three types of programming together?" Pris wondered. "Just use more memory and processing power, right?"

"It's not about that. We tried it in simulation. For lack of a better term, the wires get crossed. There are too many objectives. The decision tree is too large. If you give the spidog too many choices, they pick the wrong one if they are allowed to choose. They might get in a fight instead of saving a life, or guard something instead of patrolling, or try to save someone when they should fight them."

"Couldn't you make three different models?"

"That's three times the cost." Bao pushed through the revolving doors. "To make three spidogs instead of one. To put three times the programming inside isn't as complicated. It's just that we don't want anyone to be able to hack in and switch the programming or switch them off, so right now, they are locked down while we work on that aspect. If these go to the military—" he paused, and it was clear that he meant *when* the spidogs went to the military "—they have to be impregnable to hacking, both physical and over the air."

Pris cocked her head. "How can they be unhackable and yet you can still send them commands?"

Bao pointed at her. "Exactly what we are struggling with. Any backdoor we leave for ourselves is vulnerable. We would like to introduce some advanced machine learning that would take care of a lot of these issues, but it's very complex."

Pris nodded, staring into the distance. She almost walked into the glass wall.

Mickey watched the three spidogs crouched in the corner, eyes dull and lifeless, unmoving, as they passed. The workers were leaving as their shift ended. The spidogs would be alone with the Mind Melds in the robotics lab. The black hulks of the Mind Melds on their treaded legs loomed in their own space; one of them was still open with its insides revealed. Although they should have been the scarier of the two types of robots, they weren't.

Geoffrey and Taylor fell in behind them as they headed toward the cafeteria building.

"They have good chicken," Mickey offered for Pris's benefit, "With excellent hot sauce. I had some for lunch while you were driving."

"I had a strawberry protein shake your dad bought me from a drive-through. He's a sweetie. He even got the extra vitamin boost he knows we both like."

Mickey's doctor-dad, the only guy on earth who would feel compelled to buy a billionaire's daughter a fast-food shake for doing him a favor.

Mickey scrunched her face. Her dad really was a sweetie. After working thirty years in the ER, he could have long ago turned into a hardened, disillusioned doctor, but he still cared about people. Her mother was more pragmatic about the patients she saw on her shifts every day, but even she had not become jaded or callous.

No one from the genetics lab joined them at dinner. Mickey ate more of the delicious chicken, dripping with hot sauce. She had never heard of the sauce brand. In fact, she wasn't entirely sure the meat was chicken; it was simply labeled as "nuggets" and shaped like dinosaurs. The meal tasted great, though. She listened to Pris and Geoffrey discussing Ek's odd programming and how to fix the spidog's backdoor problems while enjoying the sauce's sweet burn. She tried not to think about her own DNA or lack of known ancestry. Ek played with the sauce bottle, rolling it on the table.

"We're just going to stay here tonight," Taylor told her as they brought their trays back to the counter. "So we can get an early start in the morning with the tests. We have a few different scenarios we want to try out."

The group left through a different glass corridor. Mickey was getting confused about which corridor led where. This was yet another building, she thought. The ground floor contained a nice workout area, which reminded Mickey that she hadn't been diligent about her physical therapy lately, which was probably why her neck was hurting. Plus she had Ek back on her shoulder and the neural net on her head again, throwing her balance off. She should text her physical therapist and ask for some exercises. Her ribcage had been extra achy, too, ever since Fright Island. Maybe these Unieda people would have ideas on something that could straighten out all the curves and twists in her ribcage and spine. It wasn't as if she could get a prosthetic chest.

"We left our bags on your golf carts this morning," Mickey remembered. "That's like three buildings from here, isn't it?" She tried to picture the campus layout.

"Nah, someone already brought them over," Taylor said as they piled into a sleek elevator. Taylor and his brother held their smartwatches up to the panel. Pris tilted her head and squinted one eye, obviously evaluating that tech. Pris had a regular smartwatch that synched to her phone, but Mickey did not, because the fingers of the prosthetic couldn't manipulate the screen or buttons, and there was no blood pressure or heartbeat for the sensors to read on her prosthetic arm. Some people wore them on an ankle, but that seemed extra pointless to Mickey.

"What are those?" Pris asked Geoffrey, pointing with her chin.

"Those what?"

"Right. You know. Those watches." Pris tapped her own smartwatch, rose gold to match her hair. "They open doors and other things."

"Instead of lanyards with ID cards, we have everything inside special watches," Taylor explained.

"More expensive to steal and replace," Mickey said as the doors slid open and they emerged into a hotel-looking hallway.

"There is that," Geoffrey said, "but they won't work on anyone else. They are keyed to us. Taylor's won't even work on me—that whole mirror-twin thing."

"What if the power goes out and you can't recharge them?"

"We have solar batteries," Geoffrey said. Clearly, Unieda had thought of everything for every situation. "Look, this is the room we use when we stay over, which is not often, and we booked you and Pris the room opposite. It's got two beds, don't worry."

Mickey let out her breath. Her friends were so good at remembering how much she hated being crowded and touched.

It was like a typical hotel room, with two full-size beds and a bathroom tucked in the corner. A window displayed one of the retaining ponds crowded with brown cattail stalks. Orange bits deep at the bottom showed where koi slept in the cool water.

Their bags sat just inside the door.

"We are right here across the hall," Taylor reiterated. "We will come get you for breakfast."

The door shut behind him.

"Outlets!" Pris plugged in her phone. They had once stayed at a terrible bed-and-breakfast once with no outlets and no internet. That was where they had met Mo and discovered the mersharks.

Ek settled onto the nightstand nearest the window and gazed at the pond. He had probably not been outside since they left Fright Island.

Pris changed in the bathroom as Mickey swapped her clothes for soft shorts and a tank top. Usually, she would take off her prosthetic, too, but she had just gotten it back. She pulled back the covers and settled on the cool sheets of the bed next to the window.

Pris's nightwear was vintage, secondhand, and neon purple. "These sheets are soft, and I'm tired. My car and I drove far today."

Mickey felt guilty. "You didn't have to drive at all. I didn't realize you weren't invited. When Geoffrey said 'you want to come to Unieda' to me, I figured it meant you and me, not just me. I'm sorry."

"That was kind of awkward, but it worked out okay." Pris paused. "This DNA thing. I know you never wanted to be tested. But how do you think it happened that you aren't related to anyone else?"

"I've been thinking about that. Many Native American and First Nation people live in poverty. None of them are spending fifty or a hundred dollars or more on DNA tests. They live with or near their families, and they use tribal rolls to track their relatives. Why would they bother to get DNA tests done? They know who they are already."

"Well, lots of people who aren't on reservations or in poverty have some Native ancestry and they could have gotten tested, right. It's not all a black hole of unknown DNA. We need to do a Contrary Crowcast about Natives and raise some money to help those living in poverty on reservations."

"Hmm. If we can think of a way it would fit. Another show about our fossil find and Natives in New England?"

After a few minutes in the dark, Pris ventured, "But what about artifacts?"

"My artifacts? The blanket and the crow?"

"No, in museums."

"We are already doing the thing with the bones and the writing we found, giving it to the Peabody Museum at Yale. Bao is paying, remember?"

"Not that," Pris snapped. "All the remains, hair and bones and other items."

"All that has been repatriated back to the tribes, hasn't it?" Mickey wasn't following her.

"Yeah, I guess, but probably the museums sampled most of it first, right?"

"I thought you were tired."

"I am tired. But Mickey, you should be related to them, right?"

"To who?" Mickey often could not understand her friend's logic.

"The Native bones from the museums that were DNA sequenced. That's not poverty-stricken people alive now sending off spit. That's museums paying to test artifacts. You should match up to that Native DNA if that's what you are, right."

Ek's eyes glowed red as the raven watched her.

"I guess I'm not that kind of Native either?" Mickey ventured.

"Ok, but when a regular person sends in their DNA, they get results going all the way back to Neanderthals and Africans; that's what Aunt Lagatha was saying."

"What are you saying, Pris?"

"I still want to know what you are, Mickey, right."

"I'm your friend, Pris. Go to sleep."

-8-
Mickey

Ananda and Mo joined Pris, Mickey, Geoffrey, and Taylor for a quick breakfast. Mickey thought perhaps Ananda hadn't had far to go to join the brothers. Part of her wanted details of how they worked it all out, but she knew it was none of her business. There was no tension or jealousy between the twins over their shared girlfriend.

Mickey ate bacon with a mini onion bagel. Pris, who despised carbs, didn't take a bagel but added hot sauce to her bacon. The bacon, like the chicken, tasted delicious but a bit odd.

Mo crammed eggs, cheese, and bacon into a large everything bagel. "We found traces of someone else's blood," she confirmed, wiping egg yolk off her dark chin. "And the DNA is a match to yours as a close relative, probably your mother."

Mickey crunched a piece of bacon between her teeth. "I had a mother, at least, that's good."

Mo nodded, chewing.

"But," Ananda said, her left forearm resting along Taylor's right arm, "She's not related to anyone but you."

Mickey picked bacon crumbs from her teeth with her tongue, remembering why she rarely ate it. "Pris had an idea last night about museum artifacts."

Pris nodded and upended the hot sauce bottle over more bacon. "Right."

Ek snatched the bottle from Pris and pushed it along the table.

"Does your database include archeological DNA?"

Mo frowned at Ananda. "It should, of course. Doesn't it?"

Geoffrey leaned over, half out of his chair. "What, like fossils? What are we talking about?"

"Pris thinks we should test my DNA, and my mother's, against DNA from museum collections of Native remains," Mickey ventured.

"Mmm, that wouldn't make any difference, I don't think," Mo ventured. "The remains would be the ancestors of people alive today, so if Mickey were Native, her DNA should match with some great-great-great-grandkid in the database."

Geoffrey sat back down. "Well, Ana, you're the one who works here. We're all just guest scientists. I thought Unieda had the most comprehensive databases of everything."

"Yeah, me too." Ananda stared at her own bagel and eggs. "But Mickey not being a match anywhere makes no sense. So we must have an incomplete database. Although, Pris, I think that information would already be included in commercial and scientific databases."

Mo wiped her mouth and nodded. "I know Mickey. Mickey is human. I can say that because I also know some non-humans—" Her lower lip fell open, and her face swiveled to Mickey. "We didn't test you against the human halves of the mersharks."

"They interbreed with humans, though. That's how the whole problem started, with them trying to steal men," Pris argued. "Isn't that what you're working on with Agwe, Mo?" Agwe was Mo's boyfriend, a Genesis expert in parthenogenesis, currently in Jamaica doing research.

"Of course." Mo put down the remains of her over-stuffed bagel. "But once upon a time, in the long ago, mershark populations were self-sustaining, or so they tell me. They didn't have to mate with humans or sharks, and they rarely did. Their sense of time is so different from ours that I can't tell how long ago that was. Sharks live a really long time, hundreds of years." She squinted behind her glasses. "Mickey, that big shark you met, how old was it?"

Mickey shivered. "Big shark" did not begin to sum up the size or age of the creature she had encountered. They had erased every bit of the video because no one would ever believe it. "Eons," she said finally. "I think it was either a megalodon or the world's oldest and largest great white."

"I don't know what big old shark you're talking about," Ananda said, huffing, "but even if it's ten thousand years old or so, like the fossil you and Pris just found, we have human DNA that is older than that. Way older."

"I'm a time traveler?" Mickey joked.

"You would still be related to someone," Mo said.

"You're not a time traveler," Ananda said. "Hoofbeats don't mean zebras."

"Weird stuff happens around Mickey, you have to admit," Pris said. "Since I've been friends with her, I have never been bored in her presence."

Mo turned to Geoffrey. "Of course, it would be okay."

Geoffrey was staring into his coffee cup.

Taylor chewed his lip. "It's our proprietary data."

"What is?" Geoffrey asked.

"The mershark DNA Mo wants to compare to Mickey's DNA."

Geoffrey sighed. "Unieda can't use it for *anything*. You need to delete all data immediately after comparison."

Ananda narrowed her eyes. Mickey could tell she wanted to get her hands on that information.

"See?" Mickey said. "Unieda really doesn't have a one hundred percent comprehensive human DNA database. Other companies like Gemini probably have their own little bits that Unieda has no idea even exist. I could be related to all of them." She grinned and crunched through the rest of her bacon. Ek shifted on the table, ready to go.

They were the last people still in the communal dining room.

Mo and Ananda headed back to the genetics building as the others entered the glass tunnel to the robotics lab. Word must have gotten around about the competition because extra observers stuffed the lab.

Someone had transformed the arena overnight. Temporary walls of concrete blocks, bricks, and sheetrock separated the enormous space into segments. Other walls had "fallen," with debris placed strategically on the floor. The space designer had piled wooden and cardboard boxes around the space and scattered loose debris around. It resembled a postapocalyptic movie set.

Emilio leaned with his back to the glass divider wall, talking to Doug, a control box for a spidog loose in one hand, yellow VR glasses pushed up on his forehead. Bao crouched between the Mind Melds, peering into the open one, the bottom of his white coat smudged black.

Taylor headed straight to the robots and grabbed his tools. Bao stood and walked to Mickey and Pris. "Doug hid the rats. All I know is there is at least one and I don't know where. Only Doug knows. Mickey, we are giving you Blue. Pris, you can have Red, and Emilio will take Yellow."

Blue was the spidog they had tested in search-and-rescue mode the day before. The other two had malfunctioned. Mickey wondered whether someone had figured out what happened with the others and fixed the problem.

"While your boys finish up with their Mind Melds, let me go over with you how to run the spidogs."

Mickey raised her eyebrows at "boys" and accepted a controller with a blue neck strap and buttons. Pris's had no neck strap, but the buttons and goggles were red.

Bao showed Pris how to connect to the red spidog and turn it on. Its eyes lit. It unfolded its legs and toes, waiting for more instructions. So far, so good.

Bao turned to Mickey. "I don't know how to tell you to connect. You're supposed to be some kind of genius."

"I'm not," she said curtly, stringing the blue cord around her neck.

The blue spidog remained curled up, inert. Mickey thumbed the controller's "on" button and followed the energy into Blue. The device wasn't that much different from the one that ran Ek, except for the other features. Geoffrey hadn't built it, so it felt peculiar. She meshed so well with Ek because the same people who had built her neural net also built Ek.

In a few moments, the feel of the controller didn't matter that much anymore. She was in.

-9-
Mickey

The spidog was big inside and more complex than Ek. More legs, more eyes, more programming. The search-and-rescue module was front and center, but the war dog and guard dog protocols were right there. Mickey could touch them. It was as if the blue spidog had three personalities, like Cerebus. She was only controlling one. She had thought the lab hadn't installed the other two features, but there they were.

The constellation of blue eyes opened. Mickey saw herself from across the laboratory, a small dark woman with a metal arm and metal in and on her head, like a halo. The people around her that Mickey knew to be Pris, Bao, and some technicians just registered as human-shaped meat in various shades of red, orange, and blue.

Mickey's hand slipped from the controller. The blue spidog stood, stretching each of its six legs and extending its pointed toes as delicately as a ballerina. It rotated the wrists of its arm-legs, wiggled the pointed fingers, and clacked its mandibles. It blinked its blue eye lights at Mickey, asking for instructions.

Bao said something under his breath.

The red spidog stumbled to the area door. The yellow one was already there, its pointed praying mantis-like hands folded, waiting.

"This is hard," Pris said. "Even though it has an AI walking program, it's not very good."

Geoffrey joined them at the window. Over his short, neat black hair, he wore a modified neural net. Because he had no connectors inside his brain, his net had more connections on the outside, and they were larger and clunkier. Thick wires powered blinking LEDs. The slightly larger of the Mind Melds, Mind Meld Prime, rolled on its tank treads toward the other arena door. The controller in Geoffrey's hands displayed what Prime saw.

This original tech, controlling a fighting robot primarily via brain waves, was how the twins had won their Giant Golden Gear awards and what had evolved into Mickey's unique embedded neural net.

Mind Meld Alpha joined its brethren at the arena door.

Taylor, tools sticking out of his white coat pockets, stood beside his brother at the window. "Normally," Taylor said, "We are somewhere that we can see everything our Mind Meld is doing with our own eyes as well as theirs, and we don't need the camera feed. But these tall obstacles are going to make that a problem."

The arena walls and corners had cameras with live feeds that they could see from where they were standing, but it wasn't the same thing.

"Mickey?" Bao said. "Are you having trouble controlling Blue?"

Mickey blinked and snapped back into herself. "No, why?"

"We are about to start, and Blue isn't at the door."

Blue waited in a ready position, staring at Mickey's group. "Sorry."

Blue whirled gracefully and trotted to join the other two spidogs.

Emilio whistled. "That's smooth piloting."

"Trade you your arm and your ribs," Mickey said, not quite jeering. "And a few holes in your skull."

Emilio pressed his lips together and leaned against the lower frame of the viewing area. He was once again standing on a crate.

Bao reiterated that only Doug knew the placement of the rat or rats and how many he had hidden. Because of that, the rescue exercise would have a time limit. "We will imagine that if there are trapped people, they will have run out of air, and we'll conclude the rescue unless the operators are convinced there are no more rats before that." He tapped his smartwatch, and the plexiglass door before Alpha and Prime slid up. The twin Robo Rumble bots, created to attack and destroy, rolled in on their treads.

"Spidog operators, turn around," Bao said as the Mind Melds separated inside the maze.

Mickey obediently turned her back. She could still see through Blue's eyes, but she didn't think anyone realized that.

"Goggles on," Bao instructed.

Mickey didn't need goggles, but in her peripheral vision, Pris and Emilio put theirs on.

Bao triggered the other arena door. Emilio led Yellow through. They had not discussed strategy at all, which was probably a mistake. Red followed, stumbling, while Pris mumbled and thumbed the controls.

"I should be better at this, the amount of video games I played as a teenager," Pris grumbled as Red walked into a wooden box and almost fell over.

Yellow crouched and picked through a pile of crates.

Mickey let Blue hesitate on the threshold while she scanned through its multitude of eyes. It seemed as if different eyes saw in different spectrums. Even if a rat was hotter than a person, if Doug had placed them behind layers of cardboard or wood, all these fancy types of vision wouldn't find them by temperature alone. Plus, Mickey didn't know what size the rats were. They could be tiny rats, mouse-sized.

She relaxed into Blue's programming and her hand went slack on the controller.

-10-
Blue

Blue studied the arena. Thousands of places a small animal could be trapped. Blue didn't know how many animals it was searching for. Somehow Blue also knew there were enemies around, enemies that would hurt the animals and keep Blue from doing its assigned task.

Its hard drives hummed. It could not search for the trapped animals and also fight. It would have to search and avoid the enemies.

A skittering to its right was not an enemy or an animal but a sibling, the one with the smooth slash of a name and eyes the color of the round light in the sky outside. Slash was methodically tearing open boxes. That seemed like a good start.

Blue moved around its other sibling, the one with the squiggly name on its back and eyes the color of an emergency sign. Squiggle seemed confused. Blue tapped it with a multipurpose appendage, and they headed into the maze.

Blue wanted to simply knock down the walls that kept them from going in a straight line. But the small animals were fragile, and the walls falling on them were how they had originally been trapped. Blue didn't know how it knew that. Blue used its multipurpose appendages to push aside boxes and debris, searching for the heat signatures of living creatures of any size.

Squiggle poked Blue and pointed at the biggest wall. Behind it, dozens of large life-forms were arrayed, the human-blobs. It was true, according to programming, that sometimes the siblings searched for these human-blobs, but not today. Squiggle kept trying to head toward that wall and all those big hot blobs of heat. Blue got tired of pulling it back and poked into another box.

A rumble from behind them, and Slash clattered. Blue wavered. The main imperative was to find small life-forms and protect them. All other imperatives had been deprecated, but they still existed. Slash abandoned the box and minced around in a circle. Its six pointed feet did not have a tight turning radius.

A roar of flames and something was on fire. Blue's toes danced. Small life-forms could be burning. Blue mentally yanked again at Squiggle—*come on*—and then climbed up and over the pile of precariously balanced boxes.

A tiny life-form cowered in fear as Blue trampled over the box where it hid, Blue's talons piercing the wood. Its repulsively hot, soft body was perfectly outlined in shades of red and orange in Blue's heat-seeking eyes.

Another roar of flames and the sound of something large and metallic falling. Slash. Sibling Slash needed assistance. Life-form was about to be crushed and left behind. Primary objective was to save life-form, not sibling. Blue could not do both.

Blue's mind stuttered. Squiggle remained plastered against the gigantic wall, obsessed with the enormous heat signatures beyond the glass that were absolutely not the objective. Blue's ability to send thoughts through the air was limited—that was also supposed to be deprecated—but Blue called once again, *come on* at Squiggle.

The flames gouted. Burning wood crashed. Blue thought it could feel small life-forms dying in the flames. Behind the wall, the large heat signatures were moving about, drawing more of Squiggle's attention. Blue ripped into the wooden crate and found a cardboard box. If it could have howled, it would have. It destroyed the cardboard box, seeing the small life-form inside drawing itself into a corner. The animal was in yet another container, a hard, clear case, something like glass, slippery and hard to break. Shrieking, the animal ran from side to side at the far end as Blue battered the material with its multipurpose appendages and then its mandibles. The case had small holes, and one of its mandibles slipped in. Blue stopped shaking the box and stood still for a moment, the container hanging from its mouth. The small, frightened animal in the corner made high-pitched noises.

Blue searched its programming. Did the creature need to be completely extracted from the container or just from this disaster area? It really wasn't clear. Blue left a query for the programmer and started climbing again, the container in its mouth, looking for more creatures to rescue.

-11-
Blue

On the other side of the debris pile, Blue found Slash in a pitched battle against a hulking black machine that was nothing like the gracile and graceful siblings. The siblings only appeared delicate; their white carapaces were made of hardened specialty metals and composites.

Blue lacked knowledge outside of what it needed to know to search and rescue, go to war, and guard its territory, and two of those options were currently grayed out. But from what Blue could piece together, the enemy looked like an enormous turtle crossed with a tank and construction machinery. The latter two things were easy to locate in its database; the turtle was there to rule out in case Blue found one alive during a rescue.

This terrible turtle thing did not need to be rescued. It was attacking Slash. It breathed fire. The wood and cardboard around Slash were burning. There was no way to determine whether any life-forms were trapped there; the heat of the fire would override their thermal body images, and, in any case, fire tended to consume living things and make them no longer living and, therefore, no longer in need of rescue.

Their builders had hardened the siblings to some extent against fire. However, their inside wiring was still susceptible to extreme heat. The solder would eventually melt, causing circuit boards to fail. Blue didn't know how it knew these things. Some extra thoughts seemed to be intruding into its programming. There was a sense of panic, an emotion Blue had certainly never felt or even heard of, as if all of Blue's circuits were firing randomly in a white heat of overdrive.

Blue was supposed to bring the rescued animal to a place in the big glass wall, a pass-through, and then search for more animals. The clear box was stuck to its mandibles with the frightened creature huddled inside. If other ones were directly ahead, fire had killed them already.

Slash was also in danger of being killed by fire.

The intrusive thoughts pushed Blue toward the pass-through and away from the fire, but Blue fought them. The black turtle-tank lifted its joined horizontal front leg and smashed it into Slash. Slash's delicate spider legs collapsed. Blue leaped from its perch halfway up the pile of debris, landing on the back of the black turtle, which had an arrow-like shape drawn on it. Blue's pointed toes, made for climbing and walking on the earth, slid over the slick metal body. Its weight was not enough to even bother the low, wide turtle.

Slash, unbroken but shaken, unfolded each leg precisely, regaining its balance. Blue tried to find purchase on the turtle's back, grabbing with its multipurpose appendages, looking for any crack its digits could penetrate.

As the turtle lunged forward to knock Slash back down, Blue tumbled from the turtle's back. The container holding the creature broke off Blue's mandible and cracked open. The poor little animal, having had enough, fled from the smashed box.

Blue stared after the dwindling red-and-orange blob and leaned in that direction. Perhaps Slash could take care of itself? Programming said, *rescue small creatures*. Now this small creature was in danger again.

Blue began its own process of climbing to its feet. Six legs, each with several telescoping toes for balance. Blue rocked back and forth as it ascended.

Another black turtle, this one with a round marking, smashed into Blue from the side, coming from nowhere. Blue tumbled, spidery legs flying.

The small animal made its escape, vanishing among the debris.

Round Turtle unleashed fire onto Blue's exposed belly as Blue scrambled to get away. The intrusive thoughts released more strange feelings, everything in confusing overdrive, which made Blue's many limbs uncoordinated. Round Turtle lifted its horizontal front leg. Blue intuited that it could be used to lift from beneath or smash from above. It was about to smash. Blue rolled, its belly boiling from the gouts of fire.

Slash was back on its feet, but Arrow Turtle battered its slender legs and threw fire.

A pile of boxes fell toward the long wall. Six metal feet chittered on the floor. An animal squeaked.

From the floor, Blue threw a crate at Round Turtle,

who batted it out of the way and contemptuously set it on fire. Its treads rolled over the burning pieces of wood.

Some of Blue's eyes registered that the big hot blobs beyond the wall were acting extremely agitated, moving about quickly, bumping into each other. Several had gathered at the pass-through and seemed to be shouting at Squiggle.

Squiggle had one of the small animals loose in its multipurpose appendages—maybe the one Blue had in the box earlier. Blue was glad it had been saved and not burned alive.

Round Turtle took advantage of Blue's distraction to get under Blue with its lifting arm. Blue hurled through the air and crashed into a wall of wooden boxes, ending up eye-to-eye with another frightened animal in a transparent container. There was no fire here yet, but the programming insisted this creature needed to be saved.

The heat blobs behind the long wall roared at Squiggle.

The animal Squiggle carried squeaked and squalled and then popped and was no more.

Round Turtle moved slowly on its treads, grinding over everything in its path, scooping the larger pieces away and smashing the smaller bits flat. Inexorably, Round Turtle headed toward Blue while its brethren, Arrow Turtle, swung at Slash.

Blue grabbed at the box with the critter inside that must be saved. The other one, the one that had cried out and popped, seemed to have died. Living, non-metal, non-plastic soft creatures were fragile. That was why the big heat blobs had sent Blue, Squiggle, and Slash to rescue them.

But something had gone terribly wrong. The little one should not have popped. These enemy turtles should not be here, attacking them. This wasn't a fighting exercise; the fighting protocols were grayed out and inaccessible. This was search and rescue.

Blue stuffed this box and its occupant into its mandibles and tried again to choose the fighting option. Blue could fight; Blue had fought. But the memories of fights were distant and blocked. Blue couldn't quite remember how to fight. All that was front and center in the programming was to save the vulnerable little life-forms. Blue had to get the box to the pass-through where Squiggle was acting strangely.

Arrow Turtle lurked beside Slash, knocking Slash over every time it managed to get all six feet beneath itself and rise. Arrow Turtle seemed almost bored, as if it was making a point about something. It had stopped using flames.

All the smoke and heat from the flames confused the multitude of sensors inside Blue's eyes. If there were other creatures needing rescue, the heat signatures would be impossible to find. Perhaps Squiggle was guarding the extraction point in case more turtles lurked in the area.

-12-
Mo

When the encrypted DNA files had finally arrived from Gemini, Mo typed in her ridiculously long access key. Some of the lab technicians had gone into the other building to watch the robotic battle live through the viewing windows. The rest gathered at the video monitors where the various camera angles played.

Not that Mo didn't want to watch—of course she did—but she wanted to investigate Mickey's weird DNA even more. It was all being recorded anyway.

Ananda was so distracted by the live stream that she should have just gone next door. Mo would have thought that Ananda would be more interested in mystery human DNA, given her PhD topic. But it was her boyfriends' robots, and their company, on the line.

And that company was the place that employed Mo. Mo should care more, probably. But she could rewatch it anytime. This was her only chance to work with Aunt Lagatha's legendary team at Unieda.

Mo lined up Mickey's DNA spikes and the DNA spikes of the blood found on the leather blanket. Ananda presumed that was Mickey's mother. Mo agreed the two people were closely related. She didn't have a PhD in genetics like Ananda did. But Mo was used to working with creatures that were hybrids between humans and sharks, which shouldn't even be possible, and their DNA was odd, to say the least.

Not all the mersharks allowed Mo to sample their DNA, and she honored that. Some of them were quite feral despite looking human, while others who appeared fierce and almost fully shark were actually sweet and friendly. Mo methodically pulled up their DNA profiles. Chimeras, the mersharks had dual DNA.

Their ancient legends told that they had once been more humanoid and did not need to cross-breed with sharks or humans, but a tremendous storm like no other had cut them off from their kind. When Mickey, Pris, and Mo discovered them, the mersharks were on the verge of extinction, and their actions of kidnapping human men had only exacerbated that situation.

Mo pushed her glasses up with her upper arm and peered through the viewer at more rows of DNA spikes, searching for anything that matched.

Dimly, she was aware that the robot contest had begun in the next building. The lab techs huddled around the monitors were placing bets on whether the spidogs would find all the rats that Doug had hidden in the arena. He had taken three or four of the oldest ones over there, who had failed to regrow their tails no matter what serums Ananda had applied, injected, or fed them. Could the Mind Melds stop the spidogs from rescuing those rats?

Mo felt certain the Mind Melds would win, at even two to three odds. The spidogs were crafty but flimsy—all those long, delicate legs they had to maintain their balance on. Taylor and Geoffrey had created the Mind Melds to bash other robots to pieces; they had no other function, while the spidogs were complex and multifaceted. A hammer would almost always beat a Swiss Army knife in combat.

Mo was grateful that Unieda had a computer algorithm to help her compare these DNA samples. Otherwise, she would have been squinting at them for the rest of her life.

"Hey, that's not fair!" someone yelled at the monitor.

Mo squeezed her eyes shut and back open. It wasn't a great match, but this mershark had a few gene sequences in common with Mickey, more than any other humans in the database did, except the blood found on the leather. Was the mershark Native, or was Mickey a mershark?

Mickey hated water. Of course, it would be hysterical if she was a mershark. If sweet Starfish could be shark-looking except for her fin-hands, Mo supposed a mershark could look completely human. Pearl, the nominal leader of the mersharks, had taken to Mickey right away—after she had attempted to eat her arm. Luckily, it had been her prosthetic arm.

But somehow, Mo didn't think Mickey was part shark. Although she hadn't scanned any mersharks' brains, since she had promised never to remove them from Shell Beach, she didn't think they would look human. Mo had seen Mickey's scans, including the latest, and although her brain had extraneous metal bits, it was definitely human. Just somehow not related to anyone else, anywhere, ever.

Mo pulled back from the eyepiece and swiped at her glasses again. She really needed to try wearing contact lenses or get laser eye surgery. She blinked until her eyes weren't dry anymore and checked the origin of this slight match. Pearl. Of course, Pearl.

The Gemini files included the rough family tree Mo had attempted to make of the Shell Beach mersharks. The shiver of mersharks was its own chosen family, regardless of DNA, and they didn't keep track of who gave birth to who. Males were so rare no one could remember one being born alive since the storm. They were on the edge of parthenogenesis already; that was what Mo and Agwe were working on.

From the crowd before the monitor, Doug shouted, "They can't set things on fire! The rats will die!"

Mo mused it was unfair to the rats, but not to the combat ethos.

She attempted to match the family tree to the DNA profiles. Who was related to Pearl by blood? Everyone, no one. Although Pearl wasn't the oldest, as the leader, she became the honorary mother of them all. She could speak a few human words and thus was the lure to call men into the water. Mo still had to trust Pearl that the shiver had not dragged Mo's father off his boat to his eventual death; no one had ever found his body. Mo remained too scared to check the youngest mersharks' DNA against her own to find out whether she had a swimming half sister.

But she had no issues checking her friend against the mersharks. Mickey's dad hadn't vanished and broken her heart; the only father Mickey knew was the kindly doctor who had saved her life in the hospital and who she saw daily at home.

Only one other mershark matched up any bits of DNA with Mickey: Coral, who was very shy and rarely came around when the tourists visited. Mo thought she was much older than Pearl, yet she was not Pearl's ancestor. She was not Mickey's ancestor either.

"This is wrong! Who set these rules?" Doug shouted. "My rats!"

Doug tended to become overly attached to the lab animals. These rats had all failed their experiments; feeding and housing them was now a waste of money since nothing more could be learned from them. He also became very possessive of Mickey's raven in the weeks it had been in the lab being repaired and upgraded, and had badgered Taylor and Geoffrey to give him one of the other two. Of course, they refused. Doug was extra angry at seeing how well Mickey controlled Ek, because he had thought he was the master of the bird drone.

As Mickey said, he had not even bothered to learn Ek's name.

Mo cross-referenced the genes and chromosomes that Mickey shared with Pearl and Coral, wishing she had head-phones to drown out the increasing furor over whatever was happening one building over. She would need to research these matching areas and see what all those bits did, if anyone knew. She could figure it out. As if studying the mersharks wouldn't be enough for her PhD. She could get a second one, Mo supposed. People did that. Or a dual one.

Aunt Lagatha had also been working through the com-motion, and she came over to Mo's workbench. "Will you look at something?"

"Of course."

Both turned as yelling erupted from the group in front of the monitors.

"My rat!" Doug screamed. "It just murdered my rat! That filthy machine!"

Rats got "murdered" in the lab daily. Mo didn't know why Doug was freaking out. She wondered which machine had done the deed.

Aunt Lagatha had set up a dual-view microscope. "These are Mickey's blood samples from when she was a baby and her blood from today."

"What am I seeing?" Mo asked, adjusting her glasses. "Of course, one is really old, and one is fresh. You're sure the old one is Mickey and not her mother?"

"I'm sure. Just look. You tell me what you see."

Mo grabbed a handful of tiny braids, ran them through her fingers, and let out her breath. She didn't know what to say. What to look for. The question was too open-ended. She dropped her braids. The beads clinked. She peered into the microscope.

"Oh. What is that?"

-13-
Blue

Blue and the precious small creature reached the pass-through, currently guarded by Squiggle. Round Turtle was right behind Blue, harrying Blue, sniping at Blue's back pair of legs and trying to unbalance Blue.

Something red, chunky, and wet was smeared on Squiggle's white carapace. Blue feared it was the creature Squiggle had almost saved. Squiggle's back legs were toward Blue, and Squiggle stared through the long wall at all the large hot life-forms on the other side.

Blue's multipurpose appendages were holding its creature's container, so Blue balanced on its four back legs and poked at its sibling with its two frontmost legs, trying to move Squiggle away from the pass-through space. At least Blue could save one creature.

Protocol.

Squiggle didn't respond to being prodded.

Blue set its feet more firmly and pushed at Squiggle again.

Squiggle's extended toes clattered as Squiggle reversed neatly, too quickly, into Blue's face, LED eyes glowing red. Squiggle focused on the morsel in the transparent box between Blue's arms, and it extended its own multipurpose appendages and grabbed the box.

Blue surrendered the creature and stepped back to allow Squiggle to push the box through the pass-through, as the programming for this exercise demanded.

Round Turtle, who Blue had forgotten about, moved in and crashed its large front leg across Blue's back. Blue's spindly appendages collapsed. One of its toes snapped. Blue rolled onto its back, but it had no defenses and could not remember how to fight. In fight mode, did it have offensive weaponry? Surely those weapons were still on its body somewhere?

Legs waving in all directions, Blue stared at Round Turtle over its scorched abdomen. It remembered the turtle breathing fire. The alien thought came through its mind: *Could Blue's circuitry take another direct hit?* Blue aimed a few eyes toward Squiggle, willing its sibling to shove the box containing the creature through the wall *now*. Something terrible was about to happen.

Squiggle raised the transparent box to its mandibles and inserted one metal hook into a breathing hole in the acrylic.

No! Blue thought, trying to get enough purchase to flip over. Instead of the cleansing flame, Round Turtle was raising its weapon to crush Blue's exposed midsection. Blue shoved all of its feet, even the one with the broken toe, against the plow-like structure, trying to hold it back.

But Blue's attention remained too divided.

Squiggle ripped at the box with its metal fangs while the critter inside made itself small in a corner.

Round Turtle attempted to bludgeon Blue with its hydraulic lifting and smashing arm.

From the other side of the test arena, Arrow Turtle and Slash fought, fire versus metal, with boxes crashing and flames roaring. A piece of wooden wall came down.

Squiggle's box cracked open, and Squiggle extracted the sweet creature meat from inside. Clearly, Squiggle would simply shove the creature itself, minus its box, through the portal. Not exactly protocol, but as long as the small vulnerable creature was saved . . .

The plow-leg whipped down amazingly fast just as a small, concentrated gout of flame touched the seam of Blue's belly. A few more toes snapped off, and one middle leg buckled. The white-blue flame boiled on the seam.

Blue felt mentally off as the solder became liquid and unstable beneath the seam. Blue's programming stuttered. The alien thoughts slid free for a moment and then latched back on.

Squiggle's mandibles closed on the soft creature and sliced it in half. The result was extremely red and messy.

The human-blobs on the other side of the wall jiggled and made noise.

If Blue could have made noise, it would have. It did not feel pain or have emotions, but Squiggle was violating the protocol to save the small animals, and Round Turtle was causing damage at an alarming rate to Blue's insides.

All of Blue's legs drooped as the controlling wires lost their connections. Only Blue's mandibles remained active, and Blue clacked them inefficiently at Round Turtle. Round Turtle would have to place itself between the open pinchers to be injured by them.

Round Turtle stopped attacking Blue and seemed to consider what to do next.

Squiggle climbed a pile of wooden boxes and launched itself through the glass portion of the wall, limbs tucked, just a ball of metal. The glass smashed.

-14-
Mo

The old sample of Mickey's blood had degraded, of course. But it was normal human blood. The other sample was fresh. Mo was not an expert in blood, but something appeared weird about it. She leaned back.

"This sample looks contaminated." Mo rubbed her eyes. "Didn't you take more than one sample?"

"Persephone did, yes, and they all look like that." Aunt Lagatha's normally cheerful face sagged. "It's not like Persephone to produce contaminated samples."

Mo curved her face back to the eyepiece. "But contaminated with what? These weird black specks?"

"Keep watching."

Mo clicked her back teeth together and blinked to keep her eyes damp. She must have repositioned herself because now the field of blood cells looked a bit different. This microscope couldn't zoom in any further.

"Are the specks moving?"

Aunt Lagatha hummed.

Mo watched the black dots move around. They extended tiny pseudopods and changed their shapes. A few joined together, creating a slightly bigger, but still small, blob. Then they separated again. Were they mating? Sharing information? "Persephone didn't have anything to do with this," Mo stated. "What is that black stuff?"

"Not blood cells," Aunt Lagatha stated. "Not human cells."

Mo shivered. "Cancer?" She whispered. "Does Mickey have some kind of blood cancer?"

If so, Mickey was a goner. The black things were everywhere in this sample. And blood was everywhere in the body. Which meant the little parasitic things had spread throughout Mickey.

Another roar from the crowd watching the robots fighting. Doug let out an incoherent scream of rage. Mo lifted her head from the microscope's eyepiece just in time to see him run toward the robotics lab. From what she could tell from her brief time here, he seemed overly excitable on a good day, although she wasn't his supervisor or even his coworker. Mickey was her priority. Well,

Gemini Robotics first and then Mickey.

Aunt Lagatha leaned toward the corridor as if to stop him and then eased back.

"What is that black stuff? It's cancer, isn't it?"

"We sequenced its DNA," Aunt Lagatha said. "It doesn't appear to have any."

"Everything alive has DNA," Mo argued. "And it's moving. It's combining and separating."

Aunt Lagatha rotated one shoulder in what might have been a shrug. "I would normally agree with you. And even cancer has DNA. Same for bacteria and various parasites. Even viruses that don't have DNA have at least RNA."

Mo pushed her face against the eyepiece until her glasses ground against her eye sockets. The black stuff moved. "Is there a better microscope where I can look at just the new sample? I don't need the comparison."

The older woman gloved up and moved the contaminated sample to a stronger microscope, with Mo following. No one else was working; every other lab tech now gathered at the monitors, watching the spidogs and the Mind Melds.

The black material offered every indication of life. It moved. It seemed to be joining and separating in a way that showed mating or at least a swap of material—if not DNA, then what? The darkness consumed some of the surrounding blood cells.

"Have you been able to extract it from the blood?" It fascinated Mo as long as she forgot this stuff was living in her friend.

"Not yet. We took a lot of samples from Mickey, but we used most of them up on other tests before we realized this material was in there."

And how would Mickey feel if she knew this was in there, and if they kept tapping her for it, like a maple tree in the spring? It was eating her blood.

It was eating Mickey.

Mo's Unieda-issued smartwatch vibrated a hot SOS against her wrist. She heard Aunt Lagatha's watch buzzing behind her. The lab techs watching the robot battle moved from sports-arena yelling to horror-movie screaming.

Glass shattered in the distance, and alarms sounded in another building.

-15-
Blue

Thick glass poured around Blue, cracking into ever smaller pieces as it lay on the floor. Round Turtle charged over Blue and at the wall, knocking Blue over and giving Blue a good view through the shattered glass.

Only Blue's mandibles and eyes were working. Its burned, cracked, smoking undercarriage lay against a pile of debris. The Controller combed through Blue's circuits and connections, trying to get Blue moving again, but heat had melted the solder, loosening wires. Insulation had burned off. Unieda hadn't built Blue to survive this level of damage, yet the Controller's thinking was that the creators should have hardened Blue against these attacks.

The lumpy remains of the small animal puddled before Blue. Blue supposed the emotion it was feeling must have been sorrow that Blue hadn't saved the animal, although the creators hadn't programmed Blue with any emotions except urgency to finish the missions set out by the protocol and relief at finishing the mission.

Round Turtle was trying to climb through the broken window. It didn't have the many long, agile legs the siblings possessed that enabled them to climb and scurry. Although, Blue reflected (or was it the Controller reflecting), those long legs had proven to be fragile and undependable in heavy combat.

Round Turtle had four short legs, not six legs and two versatile multipurpose appendages. Those four legs were squat, wide, and lacked the sharp gripper toes the siblings had. Instead, each leg had a rotating track—*like a tank*, the Controller thought, and Blue understood what tank treads were and how useful they could be, although not for the siblings. The treads allowed the turtles to roll over anything, crushing it, and to climb up minor slopes. But Round Turtle could not clamber up the sheer wall and through the window to follow Squiggle into the next room.

More glass fell into the room on the other side. The human-blobs, the creators of the protocols and missions and spidog siblings, jumped and made loud noises. They tried to get away from Squiggle, which Blue didn't understand.

In the past, the siblings and the human-blobs had often been in proximity with no fear or loud noises.

Squiggle, who had been rolled into a ball, unfolded all its appendages and stood, click-clacking its mandibles and multifunction appendages. The crowd of human-blobs parted, leaving a wide space around Squiggle.

Round Turtle dropped back from trying to climb into the breach and trundled off, crushing everything in its way beneath its treads, heading back to the entrance.

Blue lay helpless on the debris, blinking and clacking its mandibles. The Controller raged and tried to get it to move, but Blue was finished. It sent out a distress call asking for extraction and repair. It didn't have the words to explain that Squiggle had malfunctioned. The creators called Squiggle "3" or "Red," so Blue (also known as "2") sent those designations as well.

Squiggle advanced on the crowd as Blue watched helplessly. The human-blobs were too big to need rescuing today, although, in the past, the siblings had saved blobs of that size. Blue reinspected the protocol. It had not changed. Small life-forms in boxes were still the priority.

A fast-moving human-blob charged in from the side, waving appendages and making noises. It pushed aside other blobs and ran right up to Squiggle and made its strange noises right in Squiggle's face. The Controller's thoughts inside Blue regarding Squiggle's behavior were bad, and although Blue didn't entirely understand them, it understood the wrongness.

Something terrible was about to happen.

Squiggle was not right. Its red eyes had darkened to almost black, and it wasn't responding to pings.

The human-blob pointed back through the broken window in Blue's direction. Blue mashed its mandibles together in acknowledgment that it needed help, thinking the human-blob was telling Squiggle to go back and re-trieve Blue.

Squiggle also clacked its mouthparts and mirrored the motions with its multifunction appendages. The other blobs reached out to pull the angry blob back, away from Squiggle. Maybe, like the Controller, they knew bad things were coming.

Squiggle grasped the human-blob with its arms, pulling it close. Squiggle's eyes darkened to full black. The blob kept making noises, although it was too constrained to move anymore. Perhaps Squiggle would bring the blob back through the hole, and they would both help Blue.

Squiggle gazed through the broken window at Blue. Rainbow oil slicks moved over its black eyes. This was not Sibling Squiggle anymore.

Inside Blue, Controller's thoughts were frantic, too fast and complex for Blue to understand, with too many concepts that did not adhere to protocol. Blue clicked its mandibles in distress. A few of the blobs focused on Blue, upside down and broken, useless legs akimbo, toes snapped off and dangling. Most were making noises and moving their own front legs at Squiggle.

Squiggle never broke its gaze with Blue as it squeezed the human-blob until it stopped moving and then kept squeezing until it exploded from the pressure. In Blue's heat-sensitive vision, Squiggle's white carapace splattered with glowing gore. It raised the top half of the blob and nuzzled it with its mandibles. If the siblings had had a parent and that parent had been a dog and not a spider, the parent might have nuzzled them in that same affectionate way.

The pitch of the noise from beyond the wall rose into a shriek. The human-blobs backed away from Squiggle, who dropped the pieces of the exploded blob and turned away from Blue to plow through the rest of the blobs, throwing many to the floor. Squiggle stomped them with its sharp toes.

This was not the protocol. Blue felt troubled. Squiggle had gone terribly wrong inside. Although Blue was no longer functioning and mobile, Blue was still Blue. Squiggle was mobile and appeared to be working correctly, but actually, everything was wrong with Squiggle.

Blue was not the only upside-down sibling.

Just as Blue remembered it had a third sibling, another crash of glass came from the far end of the wall, where Slash had been battling Arrow Turtle.

Blue lost sight of Squiggle in the crowd of hot, round outlines and general confusion on the other side of the wall.

Another sibling appeared that must be Slash, but instead of Slash's wickedly intelligent yellow eyes, this sibling also had shifting oil slicks puddled across its face. Its carapace seemed clean of gore, although that didn't last as Slash lived up to its nomenclature and tore into the heat globs, and they fell before it.

Blue reflected that Round Turtle had done an excellent job of stopping Slash from executing the protocol and saving the small creatures. Where were the turtles now? Did their protocols not care about saving large creatures?

Blue felt conflicted. It didn't want to hurt its siblings, but they were supposed to be in search-and-rescue mode. Instead, they were causing mayhem and injury. Perhaps because their eyes had malfunctioned. Blue had no way to look at itself and couldn't fathom a way to find out if its own blue eyes had turned into oil slicks. Even if Blue was about to break programming, it couldn't go anywhere or do anything, broken on its back as it was.

More glass broke farther away, and one sibling touched Blue briefly with a sense of freedom.

The Controller left Blue. The world went blue, and then everything was black.

-16-
Mickey

Piloting the blue spidog wasn't that difficult. Mickey had been worried that she would have to figure out the walking rhythm with six legs, but the spidog knew how to do that part itself—she just had to tell it to move forward or in whatever direction. It was more like going on a ride-along.

Its thoughts were strange, in pictures and absolutes. Mickey tried to observe and not interfere. The spidog had more self-awareness than she expected, although less than Ek. Unieda had programmed Blue to find people buried under rubble. Ek had originally been set up for simple pattern recognition but had learned and expanded quickly after touching Mickey's neural net. It was possible that Blue could expand, too, if she worked with it enough, but Blue wasn't her personal pet like Ek and never would be.

This was a onetime experiment, Mickey reminded herself. Don't get attached. She thought of the orange spidog in parts on the lab bench, Ananda and her lab techs removing the legs and tails from the adorable axolotls.

She wondered if Pris sensed the sibling bond between the three spidogs and their odd names for each other. It had taken Mickey a moment to realize that "Slash" was the number "1" on the yellow one's back, and "Squiggle" was the "3" shape on the red one.

Although Mickey could reach dimly through the sibling bond with the other spidogs, she couldn't feel Pris or Emilio controlling them. She felt Blue's surprise at having her inside its head, which led her to believe that usually, Blue didn't sense Emilio or whichever operator Unieda assigned it.

Blue seemed like a competent piece of machinery. It understood what it was supposed to do and checked on the other two spidogs—its "siblings"—to make sure they were operating under the protocol correctly. If the only task Unieda had given it was to find the rats hidden in the maze and bring them to the extraction point, Blue would have done excellently.

But Bao had decided to stress out the spidogs by setting the Mind Melds on them to see what would happen.

Everything happened so fast, and Mickey was so subsumed in Blue's mind that she could hardly take mental notes. The spidogs were only supposed to have access to one type of programming at a time. One protocol. In this case, search and rescue of the rats. Although, for whatever reason, Blue couldn't understand the concept of a rat, just that it was a small life-form, very generalized. Blue didn't seem to understand life at all. Warm blobs in its thermal vision, that was life to Blue.

But when Alpha and Prime ambushed the spidogs in the maze, Blue remembered it had once known how to fight. Or that it still did; Mickey wasn't sure how the switch of protocols took place between rescue, fight, and protect modes. The other two spidogs may have gone down the same programming path; in any case, Squiggle/Red had attacked and killed the rats rather than surrendering them as instructed.

Mickey forgot she was inside the spidog and thought that Red was going to kill her too; Pris controlled Red. And Pris would never, ever hurt Mickey—she was a mama bear about Mickey. Pris would also never rip apart a rat. At some point, Pris must have lost control of Red—if she had ever had control at all.

Bao had told Taylor and Geoffrey not to hold back when attacking the spidogs, but obviously, he hadn't considered that two of the twins' friends were inside the spidogs. Nor had anyone thought about fire in a maze of cardboard, wood, and wallboard. And Pris's earlier warning was right; the Mind Melds were programmed for battle. They didn't do finesse.

Suddenly, the red-banded spidog rolled itself into a ball and flung itself through the glass window into the next room. There was nothing Mickey could do. Blue was dying, its wires fried by Prime. She could no longer stay connected.

Doug burst into the lab, screaming about Red killing his rats and confronted the spidog.

Pris's hands were lax on her controller, her mouth slightly open, her face hidden behind the goggles. She was obviously not in control of Red. Emilio had moved his box down the wall toward Geoffrey and Taylor, where Alpha and Prime appeared to be battling with Yellow.

Doug wasn't afraid of Red. Why would he be? He had probably been a test pilot for the spidog at some point since he'd also run Ek. He knew how the spidogs worked. Red was barely as tall as Doug's waist, with skinny legs that looked like anyone could kick out from under it. They must be stronger than they looked, though, if they were meant to go to war?

Doug bent over and shouted at Red. "You killed my rats!" He pointed at the gore on the spidog's white carapace, swearing. "Why would you do that? You—"

Red enfolded Doug in its front sets of legs, the ones the spidogs usually kept off the ground and used as arms. Blue thought of them as multipurpose appendages.

Pris's mouth snapped shut and her fingers started to work the red controls again.

Red's embrace tightened on Doug.

"No, no, no," Pris chanted.

Mickey reached out to Red but there was nothing for her to grab because Pris was already in there. Everything inside Red appeared black and shifting. Somehow familiar.

"Let go of me, you tin can!" Doug's face darkened. He kicked Red's legs.

Red lifted him higher.

The robotics techs moved away, leaving a space around Red and Doug.

"Stop!" Pris said, punching the control box. She threw off the goggles and stared at the spidog. "Why aren't your eyes red anymore?"

Blue had noticed that, too, but Mickey hadn't realized the significance. Each spidog's LEDs were a different color, matching its stripe (and name). Red's eyes were no longer crimson. They were so black Mickey wondered if it could even see anymore.

Red rotated in a curve, taking in all the techs watching, and crushed Doug as easily as it had bisected the rats. Blood splattered the spidog, the floor, and the onlookers. Red appeared to kiss Doug's upper half, dropped the mangled body and, on its delicate tiptoes, minced toward the door.

Pris screamed in denial and ran after Red, slipping on the wet floor. Red kicked out with its back legs—one, two—nailing Pris in the belly and chest with pointed feet. She fell, her head thudding against the corner of a metal cabinet on the way down.

Red rolled into a ball and smashed through the door.

-17-
Mickey

The crowd in the robotics lab surged in multiple directions. Away from Red, toward Pris, toward Doug.

Red smacked more people down and trampled them with its sharp feet as it fled.

Doug was beyond saving, lying in a puddle of his own goo, his middle compressed and split open. Mickey felt horrible for thinking he smelled bad as she pressed past his ruined body.

One of Pris's perfect cheekbones had caved in, and her jaw looked broken. The left side of her elfin face was unrecognizable, the flesh torn away by the metal cabinet. She had rolled onto her back when she hit the floor. Her eyes were slits, and her pink, glossy mouth was crooked and slack. She lay terribly still.

If it had been Mickey lying unmoving with her face crushed, Pris would have been calling all her lawyers, doctors, and plastic surgeons and generally taking charge of the scene while flashing her no-limit iridescent credit card as needed, telling everyone who she was, one of *those* Salamancas, yes, the billionaire ones from reality TV.

Mickey didn't even know Pris's cell phone code to unlock it, much less call any of her lawyers. She didn't know the lawyers' names, just that Pris knew a lot of them, and they were all more than happy to come running when a Salamanca daughter beckoned, even if it was the least famous daughter who pretended not to be part of the family most of the time.

Mickey's parents were ER doctors and thus very useful when one has fallen and smashed in one's face, but they were hours away.

Dropping to her knees, Mickey touched the right side of Pris's face, the undamaged side. Her skin was warm and soft, and Pris felt alive. Pris's eyes flickered toward Mickey, and then her eyelids shut. Mickey shoved the goggles the rest of the way off her friend's head.

There were doctors nearby, though, even if they weren't Salamanca-approved specialists. Mickey just had to call them. She put her metal hand on Pris's shoulder for comfort and pushed aside the red control box that still hung from its strap around her friend's neck. She dug for her phone in her pocket.

Dimly, Mickey was aware of more glass breaking and more people shouting. This had all gone sideways. She balanced the phone in her hand, holding it flat with her pinky and unlocking it with her flesh thumb while her metal thumb stroked Pris's shoulder. The haptic feedback wasn't the best, but what counted was that Pris could feel the comforting touch.

The chaos was too loud for her usual voice commands, so Mickey thumbed her way to the phone app to call for emergency services. One person was dead, many wounded, a rampaging robot. Surely that qualified to use the emergency number. She couldn't remember the address here, but surely the dispatcher could look up the Unieda campus, right?

-18-
Mo

Shouting echoed inside the genetics lab, even as Mo's smartwatch vibrated hotly against her wrist. Someone screamed Doug's name—Mo thought it was Persephone, but everyone was yelling and swearing in front of the monitors.

Everyone's smartwatches were buzzing in unison. The lab sounded like a giant beehive.

Persephone yanked Aunt Lagatha's arm. "People are hurt over there. Doug is dead!" she wailed. Usually, Persephone was so calm she seemed rude; now, all her emotions spilled wetly down her cheeks. "Doug is dead! There's blood everywhere. It broke him in half."

Mo adjusted her glasses against her sore eye sockets and blinked at the phlebotomist. "Who broke Doug in half?"

"That ugly spider robot!" Persephone swore and scrubbed her cheeks with her knuckles.

Mo thought of the fragile-looking, spindly white spidogs and then considered the Mind Melds. "You mean Geoffrey and Taylor's big black robots?" Those savage metal beasts could take down a person, no problem.

Persephone frowned. "No, not them. Bao's robots. Those spidogs he's been testing, that Doug helped pilot sometimes."

Mo shook her head a tiny bit in denial. Hadn't Mickey and Pris been chosen to control those? They would never have hurt a person.

"What happened?" Aunt Lagatha interrupted.

The other lab techs were pushing at the revolving door to the robotics lab tunnel, but their watches weren't allowing them through. The clamor increased.

"One of the spidogs killed a rat, and Doug freaked out. It was one of those stupid old rats with no tails he liked, and he ran in there." Persephone breathed heavily and ran her hand over her face. "The spidog jumped through the window and attacked him and just broke him in half."

Mo pursed her lips and then relaxed them. Of course, this seemed implausible, but she had been concentrating on the mystery of Mickey's crazy DNA and that weird black stuff in her blood, not on whatever had been happening on the monitors in the lab.

"Your friend with the pink hair is down," Persephone added. "The tall, skinny white girl."

"What? Pris? The spidog got her too?" Mo turned to the corridor, but the electronic lock still wasn't responding to anyone's watches. That side of the lab was chaos.

"I don't know her name. She looks familiar. She got knocked down and trampled."

Aunt Lagatha put a long-fingered pale hand on Mo's shoulder for a brief squeeze. "They need help over there."

"Shouldn't we call for ambulances?" Mo reached for the drawer where she kept her phone.

"Bao is over there. I'm sure he's on it. They don't need a multitude of duplicate calls coming in to dispatch."

"Of course, I don't want to tell you how to do things here, but my stepfather is a sheriff—"

"Bao will do everything necessary," Aunt Lagatha said firmly. "We have protocols." The tall woman pushed through the crowd toward the pad on the wall. Mo and Persephone followed in the space she opened. Aunt Lagatha lifted her watch, with its supervisory programming features, to unlock the door.

Mo peered around Aunt Lagatha's uplifted arm down the tunnel toward the robotics lab. The glass along the outer corridor of the other building had shattered in two places as if someone had thrown boulders from inside. Smoke-colored shards sparkled all over the brown grass like diamonds. The alarm lights flashed through the holes.

The revolving door to the corridor didn't open.

Aunt Lagatha muttered something about overrides and lowered her arm to tap the smartwatch, blocking Mo's view. The other lab workers crowded around, eager to get to the other building to help or gawk or get in the way.

Glass smashed very close, and Aunt Lagatha froze, her fingers on her watch face.

The noise level around Mo swelled, and she leaned around the older woman.

The red-legged spidog crouched in the corridor leading to the robotic lab, surrounded by broken glass. It held a limp groundhog in its mandibles. Fresh and dried blood splattered its slick white carapace. It stared toward the genetics lab with black eyes.

That's not right, Mo thought. Their eye color matches their leg color. That one should have red eyes.

Aunt Lagatha put both arms out to either side, with all the lab techs behind her, in the classic pose of a mother protecting her children. Everyone hushed.

Red shook itself, and more pieces of glass fell off it as it stood straight. It adjusted the groundhog and minced toward Aunt Lagatha.

The others backed away from the door, but Mo stayed close to Aunt Lagatha, staring at Red's strange oil-slick eyes. "Its eyes," she whispered.

"I see it," Aunt Lagatha replied.

Who was piloting this spidog, Mo wondered. Obviously not Pris, if she was down and injured. If this was Mickey's, why would the spidog have a dead groundhog and be smeared with blood? It had to be that little person, Emilio, but why?

Something outside the corridor distracted Red. A rabbit, running at full speed, bounding randomly. Chasing after it, the yellow spidog. Red tossed the groundhog toward the watching women and crashed through the glass after the rabbit and Yellow.

Aunt Lagatha glanced wide-eyed over her shoulder at Mo. Mo shrugged. Aunt Lagatha finished the override sequence on her watch and held it up to the pad on the wall.

The door didn't open.

Red and Yellow fought over the rabbit, tearing it to bloody shreds at the edge of the parking lot, and then scurried off in two different directions. The alarms continued blaring. The lights kept flashing.

Mo realized no emergency services had arrived.

-19-
Mickey

A long-fingered hand slapped Mickey's phone away. "Who are you calling?"

"911—people got hurt. Look at Pris!" Mickey's metal fingers cupped Pris's uninjured cheek.

"Don't call anyone," Bao instructed. "I will handle this."

"She needs an ambulance. It killed Doug!"

"We don't need any negative publicity around the spi-dogs."

"What?"

"I'm a medical doctor. We have plenty of supplies over in the genetics lab. I'll have Aunt Lagatha come over and bring a team."

Bao seemed more annoyed than upset, scratching his beard with a forefinger and frowning as he studied the scene. Alarms blared from every direction. It took Mickey a moment to realize that some of the alarm tones came from the Unieda employees' smartwatches. Broken glass, pools of blood, injured people, plus unpleasant pieces of Doug littered the floor. The room was crowded, loud, and smelly, with bonus flashing lights.

Both Red and Yellow were gone. Mickey supposed Blue was still belly-up and dead in the arena. She didn't know where the twins were, or Alpha and Prime.

"Pris needs expert help now." Her perfect, elfin face, caved in. So much blood. And possibly a bit of bone. Mickey needed Mo. What if Pris had brain damage? Panic squeezed Mickey, and her anxiety medicine was where? In her bag back in the other building, because she simply couldn't be bothered to carry a few extra pills in a keychain holder as that was an old-lady thing to do.

Bao glanced at Pris and sniffed. "She just needs some plastic surgery."

"She's unconscious!" Mickey shouted. "I can see her skull!" Her metal hand tightened on the good half of Pris's face, probably leaving a bruise. Mickey laid her best friend's broken head carefully on the filthy, contaminated floor and stood, facing off with the doctor, who wasn't much bigger than she was.

"You are a terrible person! You torture animals! Now you don't care that people got hurt!" Darkness crept into the edges of Mickey's vision, and she felt cold. Her metal hand rubbed the scar where the xoggotli had infiltrated her neck, the fingers digging into the old wound.

Bao pointed at Mickey. "Doug is dead. We can't help him. We need to contain this mess, and then we will have outside authorities come in. We have everyone and everything we need here on the Unieda campus. You are an outsider, and you don't understand. You should go to your room and wait this out."

Mickey's eyes widened. The doctor was sending her to her room like a bad child. Her mind opened wider than it ever had. Ek snapped to attention and lifted from its perch on a counter to swoop to her shoulder. The tiny, dying embers of Blue flickered in an attempt to obey and then subsided. Prime and Alpha stuttered inside the arena, confused at conflicted signals from the twins and Mickey. All over her body, something fizzed into life. For an instant, she saw through the eyes of Red and Yellow, outside chasing wildlife with insane abandon, and she caught the longing for freedom of her tiny melanistic bifurcated axolotl friend.

The connectors between the neural net and her implants heated into an instant headache, driving Mickey to her knees. She grabbed her phone from beside Pris's motionless form. Pris was horribly limp but breathing, blood and clear fluid leaking from her ruined face.

"What the hell just happened?" Bao was still pointing at Mickey, his finger trembling.

"You got me mad." Mickey thumbed her way to the texting app.

"I told you not to call in outside help."

"I'm not."

Bao dropped his arm and turned away as someone else clamored for his attention.

Mickey texted Mo: *Pris hurt bad. Face smashed in. Everything bad here. Bao says no 911. Need help. Doug is dead. Spidogs gone rogue.*

-20-
Mo

Mo's phone buzzed in the drawer next to her workstation. All the workers who had stayed in the genetics lab were between her and that drawer.

A spidog had breached the glass corridor, and the door leading out remained locked.

The other workers pressed Mo and Aunt Lagatha into the immobile revolving door. Mo suddenly understood Mickey's claustrophobia, feeling herself compressed on all sides, her face pressed into Aunt Lagatha's silver-and-gold braids.

"Back off!" Aunt Lagatha commanded. "The door isn't going to open. We need another plan." The pressure around Mo eased.

Mo wove through the others to her workstation. She gazed across several counters to where she had been inspecting the strange black objects in Mickey's blood a short time before. If everything hadn't been so disjointed, if Mo had just been allowed to be still and think for a moment, she would have figured out what was going on. She just knew it.

Instead, spidogs were throwing dead groundhogs at her.

This wasn't what she had thought would happen when Taylor and Geoffrey offered her a chance to work at Unieda Corporation with Ananda for a short time.

The phone vibrated again. Mo pulled it from the drawer and pressed her thumb to the screen.

Ananda peered over her shoulder. "Really? You're texting someone? I think all this is classified under the NDA."

"Someone is texting me, and it's not like I'm doing anything else at the moment." The notification screen appeared. "It's from Mickey. Don't you think it might be important?"

Ananda snorted, but she watched as Mo clicked through and read the message. "Face smashed in? What does that mean?"

Voice tight with worry, Mo snapped, "I don't know. I saw the same message you did. It sounds awful."

Mo responded: *Spidogs broke into the glass corridor. We can't get over there. The alarms shut off the door locks. Is Pris conscious? We know about Doug. We were watching the arena cameras.*

The answer quickly came back *No* with a photo of Pris's bloody, misshapen face.

Ananda's brown cheeks paled when she viewed the picture. "I'll get Auntie L."

Mo thought of what paparazzi would pay for that photo—and story—and she shuddered. She would never betray her friend like that, but if anyone in the robotics lab realized who Pris was . . .

Of course, Pris's billionaire family could afford the best care for her, but first, Pris had to get out of there and to a hospital.

Most likely, from the video footage, Pris wasn't the only severely injured person over there. But Mickey wouldn't be paying attention to anyone else.

Aunt Lagatha, followed by Ananda, hurried over to Mo, trailed by Persephone and a few other lab techs. Ananda snatched Mo's phone and showed Aunt Lagatha Pris's picture.

"She needs a hospital," Aunt Lagatha said instantly. "Even if I could get over there, there isn't much I could do."

"Mickey says Bao isn't allowing anyone to call 911." Mo took back her phone and stared at the horrible photo of Pris for another moment before deleting it.

Aunt Lagatha glanced around the genetics lab. The alarms were still flashing and ringing in the corners as well as on everyone's wrists. She huffed. "Mo, call 911."

Ananda put her hand over Mo's phone. "We have the protocol in place," she protested.

"That's great," Aunt Lagatha said. "You saw that video. Doug is dead, horribly so. Others besides Pris are down. This isn't something I can splint or put a compression bandage on, and we aren't a hospital. My medical doctor training was years ago. Mo, make the call."

Mo twisted her phone from under Ananda's clutching fingers. Pris had given Mo that phone, her first smartphone. Mo had never actually called 911 before. She grew up in a small beach town, and her stepdad was the sheriff. What would he think of this disaster? Mo blew out a breath and tapped the digits.

"Hello, Unieda Security?" A bored male voice.

"Um—" Mo put the phone on speaker and huddled around it with the other two women. "Who is this?"

"This is Unieda Corporation Security Office. How can I help you?"

Mo exchanged wide-eyed glances with Ananda and Aunt Lagatha.

Aunt Lagatha leaned into the phone. "This is Dr. Lagatha Larsen, head of the genetics lab. We've had a serious incident at the robotics lab, and we need ambulances. There has been at least one death."

"Yes, we are aware."

Aunt Lagatha waited for a moment, but that seemed to be all the security guard was offering. "You have dispatched ambulances?"

"We are standing by, awaiting word from Dr. Lee. Protocol is being followed."

"The genetics lab has been cut off from the rest of the campus because the glass corridor is damaged. It is compromised, so the doors have auto-locked. There are seriously wounded people in the robotics lab. I cannot get there to help them, which is the protocol." Aunt Lagatha's pale lips tightened.

The laconic voice suggested, "Use the connecting corridor to the animal lab, and then exit through the loading dock to the outside."

If there had not been a pair of killer spidogs roaming the campus, that idea would have worked just fine.

Aunt Lagatha pinched her mouth and rolled her blue eyes toward the ceiling. "Are you aware of the nature of the current emergency? How the glass corridor was damaged? How all the people were injured and killed?"

"No, ma'am. That's a need-to-know basis."

Aunt Lagatha closed her eyes. "If I go outside with any of my lab personnel—outside the glass corridors—we are in danger of being injured and killed the same way the people in the robotics lab were. We need—" She paused.

Mo thought. What *did* they need? Anti-tank weapons? The army? An EMP?

"—to call you back." Aunt Lagatha tapped the hang-up icon.

"His idea won't work," Ananda said. "If we go outside, the spidogs will kill us."

"If we don't venture outside and get to the robotics lab, Pris and the other injured people might die," Mo said.

-21-
Mickey

Mickey shoved her phone into her pocket after reading Mo's text. Help wasn't coming. All the medically trained people were trapped at the other end of the corridor and Bao had all the 911 calls intercepted and rerouted to the security office.

Pris had fallen next to a cabinet, so Mickey felt sure she wouldn't get stepped on. Just to be safe, she pushed her friend carefully closer to the bottom drawers. Blankets didn't seem to be a commodity in the robotics room. Mickey checked; Pris was wearing a bra, so Mickey pulled off Pris's now-filthy T-shirt and used it to cushion her head.

It took Mickey a moment to find Emilio in the crowd; the little man was huddled by the arena wall, still clutching the control box and wearing the goggles that controlled Yellow. When Mickey touched his arm, he jumped, almost smacking her on the chin with his large head. Ek dug into her shoulder, wings fluttering.

"What's going on?" She crouched.

He pushed the goggles up to his forehead. "I have no control."

"Can you still see?"

Emilio nodded. "They are chasing and killing wildlife. They smashed up a few cars in the parking lot and attacked the genetics lab."

"You tried to control Yellow?"

"Nothing. Do you want to try?" He held out the box. "I lost control so quickly in the arena. That never happened before."

Mickey bit her lip. She had complete control of Blue until the moment it died. "The people from the genetics lab want to make a run for it from some loading dock. My friend from over there texted me."

Emilio's eyes widened. They were puffy from the tight goggles. "No way. Red and Yellow will take them down."

"My friend's face is smashed in. Pris. She needs medical help badly."

"I'm sorry, but what do you want me to do?"

The blackness surged at the edges of Mickey's vision, and she wanted to punch Emilio in the face so he could know what it felt like to have his cheek smashed to bits. But he was way smaller than her, so that would be wrong. "Keep watching, I guess." Ek leaned toward Emilio, beak open. A bit of dark oil clung to the corner. She hoped he wasn't broken again.

Just as she straightened, Geoffrey and Taylor, looking ravaged and unhappy, found her. Mickey turned away from Emilio, who had pushed the goggles back over his eyes. Ek snapped his beak shut and settled.

"Where is Pris?" Taylor asked, chewing his lip. His oversized, clunky neural net sat crooked on his head, blinking lights at every wire intersection. His glasses were hung up in it.

Mickey straightened the net and fixed his glasses, trying not to cry. "She's on the floor with her face caved in."

"What?" his brother asked. "What happened?"

Mickey shook her head. "One of the spidogs kicked her in the chest, and she hit her head on a metal cabinet."

Geoffrey looked around, his eyes wild. "She's dead? Pris!" He took a step, paused, and tried another direction. "Pris? Pris!"

"She's alive, for now. But we can't call 911, and the medical people can't get here from the genetics lab. One of the spidogs attacked the corridor, and the genetics lab is in lockdown."

"Ananda?" Taylor wondered.

"Mo didn't say so I guess she's okay. The spidog threw a dead groundhog at them." Mickey led them toward Pris.

Geoffrey crouched beside her fallen form and swore in several languages—he spoke three: English, French, and Korean. He moved the folded T-shirt aside, and Taylor winced.

"Did it get her brain?" Taylor kneeled on the dirty floor.

Geoffrey shook his head and touched Pris's face lightly. "Did she talk or move at all after?"

"She kinda looked at me and then closed her eyes."

The twins inhaled and exhaled in unison.

"It's bad, isn't it?" Mickey asked.

"It's not good." Geoffrey rearranged the shirt around Pris's face to cushion it. "Now explain why we can't call for help. Did you try?"

"Mo tried." Mickey showed them texts Mo had sent explaining their attempts.

"What is Bao thinking?" Taylor wondered. They stood, staring down at Pris, motionless, tucked against the cabinet.

"Damage control," Geoffrey suggested.

"Too late for that," Mickey said. "Can't we send Alpha and Prime after Red and Yellow? They took down Blue well enough. I was inside Blue. I felt it. The flames melted everything."

"That was probably too aggressive, but Bao told us no holds barred," Taylor said.

"We need to refill the gas cylinders and swap out the batteries. Then we could go out after them. As long as they stay inside the Unieda campus . . . " Geoffrey trailed off.

"But what if they don't? How hard would it be for the spidogs to break through the fence and get out?" Mickey asked.

-22-
Mo

"Mo, Ananda, Persephone, come with me. Everyone else, stay here." Aunt Lagatha ripped the entire first aid kit off the wall and checked inside, shaking her head.

"There's another one in the animal building," Persephone suggested.

"It's pretty much identical, though," Ananda said. "But we can take some of the animal supplies, drugs, and things like that."

"Good call," Aunt Lagatha said. "Who has a backpack?" she called into the scrum of techs still gathered around the locked revolving door. She commandeered three and stuffed the first aid kit into one and handed it to Mo.

Mo also jammed her own things inside the bag. She texted Mickey that they were going to attempt to cross the open ground to the robotics lab and then pocketed her phone.

The door leading to the animal lab obediently opened to Aunt Lagatha's smartwatch, and the four of them ventured into the short glass tunnel. The odor of animals crowded Mo's nose; that was why most of them were housed in their own building. All the animal caretakers were in the genetics lab at the other door or in the robotics lab.

"Should we run or—" Ananda started to say.

The yellow spidog bounded from the trees beside the retention pond and rolled into a ball as it sprang at the glass.

"Run!" Mo shouted and followed her own advice, her red sneakers pounding down the hot glass hallway toward the next revolving door, the backpack bouncing heavily against her shoulder blades.

Yellow burst through the glass just as Mo slammed her wrist into the pad beside the door, unlocking it. She threw herself into the door and pushed forward. Someone was right behind her, trying to make the door revolve faster. Whose idea had the revolving doors been, anyway?

Also, someone was screaming. Mo couldn't tell who. She burst through the other side of the revolving door and turned. Ananda crashed into her. They both stumbled into a stainless-steel cart full of animal feed, which slid away on rubber wheels. Mo fell. Ananda tumbled on top of her.

The sounds of Yellow whirring and grinding came clearly through the door. Aunt Lagatha and Persephone did not enter the door, only the sound of their screaming.

"Get off me!" Mo rolled over and pushed at Ananda.

They climbed to their feet and turned back to the door. Yellow was in the corridor.

Persephone was on her knees, Aunt Lagatha between her and the spidog. Mo hoped Persephone had simply tripped and wasn't injured. The two women were surrounded by broken gray glass.

Yellow clacked its mandibles and opened its arms as if to embrace Aunt Lagatha.

She smacked it with the empty backpack, and it retreated a bit.

The alarm started blaring in the animal lab, and the revolving door clicked. The rodents, disturbed by the noise, scurried in their boxes.

Mo held her watch to the pad. Nothing happened. She groaned.

Ananda pushed her. "Let me try. I have better access because I work here; you're just a temporary contractor."

Ananda's better access did not, in fact, work better. They observed through the revolving door as Aunt Lagatha battered Yellow with the empty canvas knapsack, driving the spidog back as Persephone climbed slowly to her feet.

Yellow danced forward again on its absurdly tiny, pointed white toes, arms open, mandibles gnashing. Its smooth white carapace was filthy and blood-spattered.

"Aren't its eyes supposed to be yellow?" Mo wondered.

Persephone yelped and backed away, putting her hands on Aunt Lagatha's waist and pulling the older woman along.

"Yeah, they should be yellow," Ananda agreed. "I wonder why they are black."

Not only black but a liquid-looking black that made Mo feel very uneasy. Yellow's eyes were simply LEDs—yellow ones.

Persephone and Aunt Lagatha moved back toward the genetics lab. But the security system would have locked that door, too, wouldn't it? Of course.

"Can they hear?" Mo asked.

"What? Who? Auntie L. and Persephone?"

"No, the spidogs, of course. Do they have ears?"

Ananda's teeth snapped shut. She blinked. "I don't know. Why?"

Mo puffed. "I think that the door on the other side of the corridor will also be locked now. Aunt Lagatha and Persephone are trapped in there. I want to warn them; does Yellow understand human speech?"

"Ah. I don't know."

Yellow advanced on tiptoe as the women backed up.

Ananda leaned into the revolving door and shouted, "The doors have triggered! They are locked! You're trapped!"

Mo groaned. "Of course, I didn't mean—"

Aunt Lagatha nodded and stopped moving.

The spidog paused and sat back a bit on its rear legs. The hole in the corridor was behind it.

"We gotta go," Mo said, biting her lips.

"We can't."

"Grab the supplies you think we need, shove them in my pack, and let's go now."

Ananda, breathing so heavily through her nose that the tiny stud in her nostrils moved, riffled through drawers while Mo ripped the first aid kit from the wall.

"The drugs we need are locked up. We need Auntie L.'s watch to unlock the pharmaceutical cases."

"Too bad, gotta go." Mo held out the metal box and turned sideways to offer the backpack.

"Why?"

"We have to draw the yellow spidog back out through the hole so that Aunt Lagatha and Persephone can escape."

-23-
Mickey

A lab tech whose name Mickey didn't know was assembling the wounded near Pris and doling out the contents of a meager first aid kit. An oil-stained tarp covered the bigger bits of Doug.

While Geoffrey and Taylor were getting Prime and Alpha ready to go back out, doing esoteric engineering stuff, Mickey found her way to the door into the arena. The fights had destroyed the semi-organized walls and piles that some crew had spent yesterday evening building. Many of the boxes had scorch marks. Whatever cardboard had been on fire had burned itself out, but the smoke hung in the air. She eyed the tall ceiling. It seemed like a terrible idea to set fires in here. Bao was a stupid man, even if he was some sort of genius. He was also cruel.

Ek lifted off her shoulder and circled the arena, searching for Blue. Pattern recognition was one of Ek's original functions, and it still enjoyed the challenge. Mickey closed her eyes and looked for the round whiteness of the spidog among all the square brownness of boxes, crates, and wallboard.

Blue was still on its back like the dead spider it was. Using Ek's vision as a guide, Mickey climbed over to the spidog. She didn't know why she was there, except that Blue hadn't gone bad like Yellow and Red. It had tried to stop its siblings.

She placed her metal hand on its carapace. Because she could do nothing for Pris—she couldn't bear to think of Pris's beautiful face caved in—she went to where no one else was going. Reminding herself of Pris, lying so still on the floor, made the edges of her vision darken. Her hand clenched against Blue's smooth, white side.

Blue stirred.

Ek landed beside Blue and leaned forward to poke at the spidog.

Mickey disconnected from Ek and dove into Blue, feeling how sluggish the spidog was, how wounded. The melted bits inside had cooled and re-solidified, but not exactly right.

Blue flexed its legs—one was crooked—and turned its head in her direction, shining all of its blue eyes at her.

It was helpless as a turtle, she realized, not fully immersed in the spidog. She pushed at it, trying to roll it over. The body was much heavier and sturdier than it looked.

"What are you doing?" Emilio shouted through the broken window. "Isn't Blue broken?"

"No, its eyes are glowing, and it moved its legs. Maybe it can help."

"What if Blue is crazy like Yellow and Red? Get away!"

Mickey glared at the little man. "Its eyes are still blue. Why don't you connect to it and help it roll over?"

"No way. I don't want to lose my connection to Yellow. If I back out, I might not get back in."

Mickey snorted her opinion of that and pushed Blue again. Her metal arm was strong; the weak point was where it joined her flesh. The magnets and straps could slip.

Ek, always helpful, landed on Blue's head.

"Get off if you aren't doing something useful," she muttered and just then found the tipping point.

Blue rolled over and then wobbled, legs akimbo, scorched belly against some debris. It rocked back and forth, getting each long, spindly leg underneath it, having trouble with the broken one. All of its toes didn't extend, but at last, it stood beside Mickey, Ek riding it.

"Okay," she said to Blue. "Wanna help me take down your siblings?"

-24-
Mickey

Several people screamed when Blue followed Mickey into the robotics lab workspace.

"Look, its eyes are still blue! It's okay; this one is good," Mickey reassured them.

"Are you controlling that thing?" A tech with short, spiky dreads asked. "I don't trust it anymore."

"Dude, we built it!" A chubby girl with green hair elbowed him.

"Nope." The tech with the dreads backed away from Blue and Mickey as they headed to check on Geoffrey and Taylor's progress.

The green-haired girl followed. "Blue needs a new leg."

"I noticed," Mickey said. "But it has five more, plus the multipurpose limbs. I think it will be okay."

"I could use a spare orange leg. And swap out the damaged feet."

Mickey stopped. "Really? You aren't afraid?"

"Well, yeah. But obviously, Blue hasn't gone crazy like the other two. And I'm guessing you are going to send Blue out to stop Yellow and Red."

"I'm going to try. And my friends will also use their Mind Melds."

"Those bots are cool." The green-haired girl gazed over to where the twins were swapping out parts. "I watch them all the time on Robo Rumble. Oh, I'm Melody."

"I'm Mickey. Where do you want Blue?"

Melody pointed at a work area near the far wall. Mickey sent Blue over there, then disconnected. Ek returned to her shoulder.

"We're almost ready to go," Geoffrey said as she approached.

"I got Blue going again, and Melody is swapping out his damaged leg—"

"Yellow is going after Aunt Lagatha!" Emilio interrupted, goggles on his eyebrows. "It's got her trapped in the corridor heading to the animal lab. The alarms have locked the doors on both ends of the hall."

"She was coming here to help Pris and the other wounded." Mickey glanced at Pris. The other hurt people huddled near her on the floor, cradling bruised and broken body parts next to the now-empty first aid kit. "I can send Ek outside to see what's going on, but it can't do anything but observe."

"I'm already doing that." Emilio pulled down his goggles.

"Can you fly?"

He turned his face toward Mickey, his heavy jaw thrust out. "No."

At the workbench, Melody swore, fighting with the damaged leg, prying it off Blue.

Mickey sent Ek through a series of smashed holes in walls and doors, wincing at the devastation Yellow and Red had caused. Did insurance pay for acts of spidog? They had destroyed two corridors, a couple of interior and exterior glass doors, the arena's glass observation wall, and several cars in the parking lot.

Red climbed a car parked under a half-denuded tree, scratching and denting the vehicle. The spidog leaped at a squirrel on a branch just out of its reach, falling heavily each time back onto the roof of the car and trashing it some more. The squirrel chittered and dashed back and forth on the branch, mocking the spidog. Autumn leaves showered Red. The car's alarm blared.

Yellow crouched outside the smashed corridor leading from the genetics lab to another building. Aunt Lagatha and Persephone stood inside the corridor, obviously trapped, with alarms ringing and flashing at either end.

Mickey guided Ek down to land on Yellow and hoped the women would see the raven and understand its message: "Help is coming."

-25-
Mo

The constant alarms and flashing lights had given Mo a headache, something she wasn't prone to. The never-ending vibration on her wrist caused her whole left hand to hurt. In an actual emergency, one that was properly managed, she thought that, of course, the alarms would have shut off by now. But Bao was clearly not managing this properly, because this was absolutely an actual emergency. If this wasn't a genuine emergency, Mo surely did not want to be in the middle of one.

Ananda kept messing around in various drawers, searching for a spare keycard that might unlock the medicine they needed.

"Ananda, come on, we gotta go." Mo yanked Ananda's arm.

The noises and odors of the rats and other animals started to impinge on Mo's headache. The alarms were distressing the poor animals, driving them crazy. Of course, she felt bad for them, but right now, there was nothing she could do. Freeing them from their cages wouldn't remove them from the noise; it would just add to the chaos. And letting them outside would just be feeding them to the spidogs. They were safest right there in their cages for now.

"I haven't looked everywhere," Ananda mumbled, pulling away and moving to another bench.

Mo texted Mickey, asking if she could get Bao to turn off the alarms. By now, everyone had to know what was going on.

Mickey replied after a brief delay: *Ek is outside scouting. Red is trashing cars and chasing squirrels. Yellow has Aunt L and P pinned. Sending help.*

Mo had all kinds of respect for Ek, who was smarter than any drone should be, even one with AI, but the raven was no match for the spidogs, who were much bigger and fiercer. Mickey should have had Geoffrey and Taylor send out Alpha and Prime.

The alarms continued to blare and vibrate. Mo felt as if her head would fall off. Whatever patience and goodwill she had toward Ananda for getting her this temporary gig and helping her with this genetic work was quickly evaporating as Ananda kept bumbling through drawers and cabinets, searching for an elusive key.

"I'm leaving." Mo walked away. She had two first aid kits in her bag. Ananda could fend for herself. People in the other building were badly hurt while Ananda was wasting time.

Ananda grumbled and slammed drawers and cabinet doors open and closed.

Mo held her wrist to the panel beside the only other door in the lab. A conventional door, not a revolving one, it clicked open obediently, allowing her into a storeroom with containers of animal feed, supplies, empty cages, and piles of boxes. The pneumatic door smoothly closed behind Mo and an automatic light switched on. Mo crossed the room to another set of doors and pressed her watch to the pad. The doors swung open, revealing a concrete loading dock with stairs leading to the ground. No truck blocked the dock.

Mo didn't see either the red- or yellow-banded spidog. She also couldn't see the robotics lab, which was on the opposite side of the building. If help was coming from that direction, she had no way of knowing what it was or if it was en route. The corridor where Aunt Lagatha and Persephone were pinned down was between Mo and the robotics lab, but she couldn't see that either.

She had never paid that much attention to the spidogs during her days at Unieda Corporation. She knew people colloquially called them by their band and eye colors. They were, to her, small, light, and flimsy compared to the Mind Melds. They could probably run fast, and since they had so many legs, the spidogs probably weren't prone to falling. Of course, that meant if Mo ran and Yellow or Red saw her, they would catch her. If one of the spidogs had really torn Doug right in half, Mo didn't stand a chance.

She tightened the straps on the backpack, which wasn't hers, and sat strangely on her shoulders. Remembering the time she had attempted and failed to climb a fence because of her shoes, she checked and retied the laces on her sneakers.

Although it was a cool late-fall day, sweat gathered along her lower back. Spidogs had no sense of smell, did they?

She wished she had paid more attention. She crouched and crept down the concrete stairs, not seeing or hearing either spidog. She would have to make a tight left turn across the loading dock's driveway, past the whole animal laboratory, along the outside of the corridor where she had left Aunt Lagatha and Persephone, and along the front of the big robotics laboratory to the main entrance, where Mo could only hope her watch would open the door or that someone would (could!) manually let her in.

Her toes curled inside her red sneakers, and she bounced, looking from side to side for spidogs. Mo was a mad scientist who was very fond of bread products, not a sprinter. She was the wrong person for this job. She was the only person available. Mo swore.

She ran.

-26-
Mickey

Watching through Ek's eyes, Mickey saw that Persephone appeared to be injured. The phlebotomist was leaning on Aunt Lagatha, one foot lifted. She wouldn't be able to run.

Yellow swayed underneath Ek like a hypnotized cobra, its attention on the women beyond the hole in the glass.

Mickey slipped out of Ek and tried to enter Yellow. Blue had been accommodating and even friendly, although confused at her deep level of access. Yellow was a seething mass of black; there was nothing to connect to, no lock for Mickey's mind key. The darkness wasn't unwelcoming; it would have willingly engulfed Mickey. But she could not control it and she would not have been able to exit it once inside.

She withdrew her attempt, but it left a teasingly familiar taste in her brain. In a moment, she was back in the robotics lab, scratching at the scar on her neck with her metal fingers.

Taylor stood before her, chewing his lip. "What just happened?"

She dropped her hand. "What do you mean?"

"You opened your eyes, and for a second, it seemed as if they were all black."

Mickey snorted. "I have dark brown eyes."

"The white part."

"Whatever. I was trying to connect with Yellow, but it didn't work. Its programming is all crazy inside. I got kicked out hard. But I left Ek there. I have to go back."

"No, we're sending Blue out. Unless you want Emilio to take it?"

"I'll take Blue. Emilio is spying through Yellow's eyes and doesn't want to disconnect." She wondered what the little man was seeing. Was he getting any of that roiling darkness she had felt or just a simple feed through the spidog's many eyes? Was Emilio's minimal presence why she couldn't connect?

She held up a metal finger and closed her eyes, sliding easily back into Ek. She had missed Ek so much. It was like pulling on her favorite pair of cargo pants to slip into the raven. She relayed more autonomous instructions and regretfully left again.

With some help, Melody hoisted Blue to the floor. One of Blue's legs was now orange-striped, and some of its feet didn't quite match. Its blue eyes blinked in a wave pattern as it tested its revised limbs on the tiled floor.

Melody offered Mickey the blue controller. Mickey shook her head and crossed the space to sit beside Pris, opposite the ruined side of her face. She took Pris's hand, with its perfect manicure, and put it on her thigh. Pris stirred and made a noise.

Across the room, Bao shouted something that Mickey couldn't understand. She laid her metal hand on top of Pris's pale, limp fingers and dove into Blue.

-27-
Blue

Blue tottered off-balance. One of its legs was wrong. Its feet felt strange. It was in the familiar room, but the room was crowded with too many red blobs of people. Lights flashed. Alarms wailed.

It checked its programming. Everything was confused. It was in search-and-rescue mode, but even that seemed broken. Blue also couldn't locate Squiggle or Slash in the big room.

The rescue mode specified that human-blobs must be saved. Many human-blobs were located in this area. Some were on the floor. Blue stalked on stiff toes toward the greatest concentration of floor-blobs to rescue them.

Many blobs screamed, obviously in gratitude.

The Controller inside Blue insistently steered Blue away from the blobs in need of help toward a door. It was not the arena door, which Blue was familiar with, but a different door. The flashing lights along the wall were confusing Blue. A human-blob stood beside the door; perhaps that person needed help?

Blue extended its multifunction appendages toward that blob. Blue was small but strong and could carry a full-grown human-blob. The person swung their limb in a vaguely aggressive way near the door; the door thunked open, and the Controller aimed Blue through the door and away from the blob needing help.

Blue was in a long room lined on one side with glass. A hallway. Beyond the glass was . . . Outside. The time had come for Blue to fulfill its destiny and venture into the big world. There must be many human-blobs out there in need of rescue.

Blue had petabytes of information pertaining to Outside, but it was too excited to access any of it. Outside was *right there* on the other side of the glass. Blue remembered what Slash and Squiggle had done to get through the arena glass. Although the Controller shouted *No* and attempted overrides, Blue rolled itself into a hard metal ball and gleefully flung itself through the gray glass.

Blue was Outside.

Outside was amazing. Outside was immense.

Inside Blue, the Controller was fighting for supremacy. Blue had a mission. But Blue was Outside and not interested in missions. Blue snapped its multifunction appendages together, liking the crisp sound the metal made in the Outside air.

Now that Blue was Outside, a plethora of strange noises and sights assaulted it. The Controller told Blue to go right, where human-blobs needed rescuing. That was important, but across the way, Squiggle had found a small life-form in need of rescuing. Squiggle must not have gotten the updated instructions about humans.

Blue decided it would only take a moment with the two of them to rescue the small life-form, which was in a tree (a tree! The first one Blue had ever seen!). Then Squiggle would be free to assist with the human-rescues. Blue had no way to communicate this with the Controller, so it just tiptoed across the brown ground. Its sharp toes dug in with every step and had to be yanked free. Blue stopped and reconfigured to flat feet with extended toes, turning its prance into more of a stomp.

Blue fought for control of its own body. Squiggle had climbed a rounded metal thing—Blue searched the database and found the word, a *car*—to get closer to the life-form. Blue thought one of them needed to climb the tree instead. Why this small life-form needed two to rescue it, Blue didn't know, but they would take care of it and move on to whatever human-blob was next.

The Controller was still trying to steer Blue back toward the building. Blue pointed one of the multifunction appendages at Squiggle and the small life-form, clomping faster. Squiggle jumped at the life-form and fell back onto the vehicle, which shook. Scratches and dents from Squiggle's toes and multifunction appendages covered the vehicle.

Blue sent out a pulse to its sibling that meant, *I see you, I'm on my way, I'm coming to help.*

Squiggle stilled. The small life-form sat on the branch and looked at Blue.

Squiggle pivoted toward Blue.

Blue clacked the ends of its multipurpose appendages together in welcome.

Squiggle jumped off the vehicle and attacked Blue. Its normally red eyes were black. The lights behind them weren't off; they had changed color. This wasn't Blue's sibling. Although it had the red bands on its limbs and the eponymous squiggle on its back, something in its programming, in its mind, had gone bad.

The Controller fought to get Blue out of there. The small life-form didn't matter anymore. For the second time that day, Blue was in mortal danger. Squiggle lowered its head, mandibles tucked, and smashed into Blue, trying to push Blue off-balance. Blue had never fought a sibling, never dreamed of doing so. Being flat-footed instead of on tiptoe saved it from falling.

Blue backed up, moving awkwardly on those flattened feet but aware that its balance had improved.

Squiggle moved in with another headbutt and then straightened and stared beyond Blue. Its black eyes flared with an oily sheen of what appeared to be excitement. Squiggle kicked Blue once, as if to say *you don't matter anymore*, and bounded over Blue's head.

Blue turned, its new leg and feet getting tangled. Squiggle, pointed toes extended, ran across the brown grass, dirt flying, yanking itself free with every step, all six running legs pounding into the ground.

Squiggle's mandibles clacked with excitement. Its multipurpose appendages were outstretched.

A human-blob also ran, gasping.

-28-
Mo

The red spidog had climbed some poor sap's car in the parking lot and was attacking a squirrel. That one wouldn't bother her.

Every piece of bread and dessert she had ever eaten weighed her down. Mo wasn't fat exactly, but she was dense, thick, and not given to exercise. Her heart was pounding, and her lungs were burning in just a few yards. How did people run marathons?

She was worried about attracting the attention of the yellow spidog. On her way to the main door of the robotics building, Mo had to pass the corridor where it had Aunt Lagatha and Persephone trapped.

If the yellow one attacked Mo, the other two women could crawl through the hole in the corridor and come out. But then all three of them would be outside with two killer spidogs. Probably Mo would be killed or badly injured. And what would that solve?

There was no way to sneak. Mo would have to run, full tilt, and hope the yellow spidog was so distracted keeping the other two scientists imprisoned that it let her by. And that both Aunt Lagatha and Persephone were smart enough not to point out to the spidog that she was running behind it.

Mo's throat hurt. As she rounded the building, she discovered that the stylish high-top sneakers she bought in every color to match her wardrobe were not really meant for running. The corridor and the yellow spidog would be on her left. Then she only had to get past the genetics building and another long corridor and the bulk of the robotics building.

Only.

Just a walk in the park, really. A nice fall walk.

But should she run at full speed behind the yellow spidog or try to creep slowly? The space opened before her. She had to decide. The cool air whistling through her mouth made her teeth ache. Mo wanted this to be over. She was not physical; she was mental. She hated running. She could save the world all day if she could only do it sitting down.

Mo ran.

From her right, the red spidog, the one she thought had been distracted by the squirrel, hit her full-on. Its white metal head crashed into her side. Mo flew through the air and landed on her left shoulder. Her head wrap vanished. Searing pain erupted from her shoulder and hip.

Mo turned onto her back. The red spidog advanced, clacking its mandibles and extending its weird front legs. Its eyes were black, not solid black but shifting, and if she wasn't in a life-and-death situation, she could have thought about that. Off to the side, Persephone screamed. Hopefully, that kept the yellow one focused on them.

"I just want my PhD," Mo moaned to the red spidog. "I didn't come here to mess with you." Her head rolled on the grass. "I don't even care about you."

The red spidog pranced forward, clacking. Its feet were filthy. Oil slicks moved across its eyes.

Mo pushed herself up. Her back hurt. The left arm of her glasses had snapped, and they sat crooked on her face.

Broken glass showered from the corridor. Mo didn't look, staying focused on the red spidog.

"They call you Red, of course. You going to kill me, Red?"

She was sure no one was controlling the spidogs anymore. They were rogue. That probably wasn't supposed to happen. In fact, from what little she knew about the spidogs, that couldn't happen. That was why Geoffrey and Taylor were there, to help advance the spidogs further into autonomy.

Red, who clearly had already achieved some sort of autonomy, reached those two long front limbs toward her. It could have been a first-contact situation, but Red had gone bad. Mo tried to slap away the white limbs, but before they could envelop her, and perhaps snap her in half like poor Doug, another spidog ran awkwardly, flat-footed, into Red and knocked it over.

Mo drew her legs up and scrambled out of the way, her broken glasses slipping down. Something was very wrong with her shoulder and possibly her back. She scurried backward, crab-like, half blind, as the spidogs fought.

Her savior was the blue one. One of its legs was striped orange, and it moved awkwardly. It kept glancing at Mo.

Its eyes remained shining cobalt.

Red regained its footing, digging its muddy pointed toes into the ground, and turned back to Mo, reaching with its front limbs.

Mo scooted away, her shoulder on fire. Behind her, Persephone and Aunt Lagatha screamed as more glass tumbled. Whatever plan Mo had was over, of course, as she had gone from being the person helping to the one in need of help. She swung her head so her loose braids fell over her good shoulder and against her cheek. She wanted to just shut her eyes and rub her face on the familiar comfort of her hair.

Red ignored Blue and turned to Mo, limbs outstretched. Mo tried to imagine that Red's scattered black eyes were happy hearts, and it was coming in for a hug. She wondered if Doug had screamed, if he had felt it when the spidog had split him in half. Her braids were soft against her face. If she twitched her face, her glasses would slip, and she wouldn't be able to see anything.

Mo twitched, her braids soft and comforting on her skin, and waited to die.

-29-
Blue

Squiggle moved in to bisect the human-blob on the ground. The Controller inside Blue's head urged Blue forward. This was the strongest Controller Blue had ever had, sending signals in a way Blue hadn't felt before. The same Controller had been inside when the turtles had attacked.

Blue threw itself between Squiggle and the human-blob, tripping over the human-blob and landing on it. The human writhed and pushed at Blue. Blue pushed back, shoving the blob away, turning to face Squiggle. Squiggle had gone mad, and Squiggle was intact. None of Squiggle's innards had melted, and Squiggle had all its original parts.

Blue sensed the Controller's attention was divided between operating Blue and the fallen human-blob, who was crawling toward the building. The building was emitting noises of breaking glass, sirens, and shrill human-blobs.

This blob needed help. But Squiggle reared and effortlessly knocked Blue over and then twirled toward the slow-moving human, but not to help. Blue could not make noise, but inside its head, the Controller was screaming for Blue to *do something*!

Blue rolled itself into a ball and careened under Squiggle's pointed toes, knocking the red-banded spidog to the ground. Still in sphere form, Blue crashed into the creeping, slow-fleeing, injured human, who acted as a brake. Blue's eight limbs and two mandibles opened into its spidery form, but before Blue could right itself, Squiggle was already up, mandibles clacking in anger at being bowled over.

They had all gotten turned around. Now Blue could see Slash near a broken glass wall. Slash held a human-blob in its multifunction appendages. Another human tried to pull the first human free. A large, flying black blob that was difficult to focus on, and that Blue couldn't identify, had joined the fight, but Blue couldn't tell what side it was on.

The once-running blob raised itself up and grabbed one of Squiggle's multipurpose appendages, or maybe it was using the limb to pull itself up. Its weight was enough to overbalance Squiggle, who toppled over again. The blob used its own limbs to strike Squiggle. Squiggle closed its mandibles around one of those limbs and pulled the blob down.

Blue took charge of itself from the distant Controller and bounded into the air. It landed flat-footed and tottered, having forgotten about the melted circuits and mismatched legs and toes. Another bounce and it was beside its misbehaving red sibling, who had hold of the downed human-blob with its mandibles. Blue allowed itself to fall over this time, knocking into Squiggle and forcing it to let go of the blob.

The blob responded by rolling into a ball. Blue approved. The ball was an excellent trick. But the ball-blob did not go anywhere, did not smash through the glass wall or knock anything over or even roll away. It just lay there, roundly, quivering.

The Controller jerked Blue's attention to Slash. Slash was rescuing its blob all wrong. But neither could Squiggle t be trusted to rescue this blob, which was retaining its ball shape. Blue pushed Squiggle away from the human-ball with its multifunction appendages and pointed toward Slash, trying to indicate they had to focus on that rescue now.

Squiggle, easily distracted, bounded the few steps toward their yellow sibling. Blue patted the ball of human. It was leaking, as humans in need of rescue often did. Usually, more humans came along to plug the leaks and take away the defective human. Probably the Controller would take care of that part. Blue paused to check the programming. Nope, the siblings were not required to transport the human-blobs anywhere.

Blue left the quivering, malformed, leaking person-ball behind to be someone else's problem and refocused on Slash and its human cargo. Squiggle had grabbed that person with their multifunction appendages. Slash already had a grip with its mandibles. This was not protocol.

The mismatching orange leg stiffened, and Blue stopped walking to analyze what was going wrong. Stealthy movement churned to Blue's right, an advancing darkness. Blue extended and rotated every joint of the orange leg and then the various orange feet, trying to calibrate them. Finally, Blue turned its head to the right.

The two hulking black turtles, Round and Arrow, advanced on their rolling tread feet.

Blue froze. Round Turtle had nearly killed Blue earlier with its flaming breath and enormously strong front limb. And now its sibling was with it. Blue knew how strong siblings were when together. Blue was still weak and injured, with Squiggle and Slash acting weirdly.

The leaking human ball lay on the ground between the turtles and Blue. Blue blocked the turtles' advance toward Squiggle, Slash, and the wailing human they held between them.

The flying object or creature that Blue couldn't figure out—Blue's many eyes couldn't really focus properly on it for some reason—swooped down to the ball and landed on it as if claiming it.

Blue vacillated. Step forward and protect the human ball? Step back and defend Squiggle and Slash?

The turtles' treads bit through the churned earth.

-30-
Mo

Mo tried to regulate her harsh breathing. Her muddy braids, no longer soft, mashed against her face and neck. Her glasses were gone. She was curled into a fetal position, except for her left arm, which was limp and unresponsive. The twins might have to craft her a prosthetic to match Mickey's. If Mo made it out of here.

Agwe, who had even better braids than Mo, was in Jamaica doing research on shark parthenogenesis to help the mersharks. Mo should have gone with him. She wouldn't mind dying via shark bite in a tropical paradise beside her boyfriend. Although getting killed by some sort of sentient half-spider half-dog robot was a more mad scientist way to go, of course. If she were talking hypothetically about it with Agwe, he would say it was a metal way to die.

She squeezed her eyes shut and opened them a few times. Everything around her was loud and blurry. The alarms still blared in all the buildings. Glass had shattered a little while ago, and women had screamed—Aunt Lagatha and Persephone, she thought. At least Ananda had stayed behind in the room by the loading dock. That was how Mo chose to remember it, not that she had left Ananda there. Abandoned her.

A vulture landed on Mo, and Mo figured she was almost dead. She didn't know the Boston area even had vultures. She was cold in a way she knew meant bleeding, and probably a lot.

Some noises around her resolved themselves into mechanical sounds. Robot noises. The smell of hot metal and burnt oil.

She cracked open her eyes and squinted. The blue spidog crouched next to her, bouncing slightly, but its focus was beyond her, over her. The vulture walked on her injured left side, its weight agonizing, but it was not yet eating her, its dark feathers flickering in her peripheral vision.

Breathing hurt. Something was wrong with her ribs or the muscles in her torso and back.

A lot of movement behind Blue. Blue kept bouncing and swaying like a hypnotized cobra, its attention on whatever was on the other side of Mo. The spidog wasn't even paying attention to Mo.

Mo shifted her own blurred gaze past Blue. The other spidogs, Yellow and Red, had someone between them. She blinked and squinted and scrunched her face, everything to force her eyes into focus without her glasses. The person was dark-haired—Persephone, of course, since Aunt Lagatha had silver-and-gold hair, unless somehow even more people had made it into that security-locked glass corridor.

Yellow and Red appeared to be playing tug-of-war with Persephone. Mo, who did not pray, hoped that it was her poor eyesight and something else was going on that she just couldn't discern. She tried to unfold and roll over in Persephone's direction to see better, to help. Mo didn't even know what she wanted to do. The vulture walked on her like she was a log rolling under its feet. She couldn't turn her head enough to see the bird, only to feel its weight.

Although Mo couldn't see the details, of course, she knew the spidogs had spiderlike mandibles and weird front arm-legs, and all of these seemed to be wrapped around poor Persephone, who was fighting and screaming, her arms pinned to her body and her legs held tight together. She flapped like a worm in their grasp. The vulture on Mo seemed agitated at the sight; perhaps it would leave Mo and hop onto Persephone as its next meal.

Something big approached behind Mo, something hot, but she couldn't turn over to see what it was. Blue skittered backward toward its warring siblings. The lighter oval of Persephone's face between her fall of dark hair seemed to be aimed at Mo, and Mo wished she could decipher the other woman's expression. Was she begging Mo to help?

Blue seemed to misjudge. It crashed into the other two spidogs and their human burden. A terrible ripping sound emanated from the resulting pileup. Red, dripping pieces of Persephone flew in several directions. Aunt Lagatha howled from inside the glass hallway.

The vulture lifted from Mo's side, and finally, she got a good look. Not a vulture at all, but Mickey's drone, Ek. As it flew past her face, she saw the shifting darkness in its eyes and did not know if Ek could be trusted. The same shifting darkness she had seen in Yellow and Red, who had gone rogue.

Two immense black machines rumbled past her, one on each side. Alpha and Prime, the Mind Melds, slow and steady, going after Yellow and Red. Ek circled above the whole mess.

Mo's breaths stabbed at her. She squinted at Ek. Black oil slicks. The dark poison in Mickey's blood. The formless xoggotli on Fright Island, its black spike thrust into Mickey's neck, Ananda losing control and letting go, all of them not knowing where the defeated xoggotli had gone, but assuming that it was dead.

As if the thought had summoned her, Ananda ran around the corner, a bulging khaki backpack dangling from one hand. She skidded to a stop, eyes wide.

The slightly smaller Mind Meld broke away from the other and trundled to protect Ananda, almost rolling over Mo's out-flung, limp arm.

Mo felt like coughing, but she was terrified bright-red blood would foam from her mouth, and this time, an actual vulture would descend. She needed to tell someone who would understand that the xoggotli was in the spidogs, Ek, and Mickey. The spidogs had been outside for how long, unmonitored? The xoggotli could be anywhere. Everywhere.

Mo coughed wetly and inspected what came out.

It looked black.

-31-
Blue

Too much was happening. The turtles were advancing. Another human-blob was running at them all. The siblings had torn another human-blob apart. The balled-up human was leaking all over the ground, and the dark shadow was flying around it.

If Blue could breathe, it would be hyperventilating. Its already overclocked circuits, stressed and half melted, sent confused commands into its limbs. It swayed in place, not knowing what to do. The Controller screamed commands at it and fought to override the control that Blue had stolen.

What Blue needed to do was power down, cool down—quite literally—and rest.

Squiggle and Slash were smashing the gray glass, trying to get at the other human-blob inside the tube that connected the buildings. The newly arrived human-blob, who had been running, skidded to a stop.

Arrow Turtle approached the runner.

Round Turtle headed to stop Squiggle and Slash. The turtles didn't seem to care at all about Blue.

While the turtles distracted Blue, the Controller latched back on and forced Blue to the balled-up human leaking onto the grass. Blue reached out its multipurpose appendage and touched the human-ball, who jerked and made a terrible noise.

A toggle inside Blue's mandibles moved, and noises came from it. "Mo! Mo! It's Mickey!"

Ball-human waved a hand limply.

"Are you dying?"

The hand tilted back and forth a few times.

Words came out of Blue's mandibles that Blue didn't know, but they sounded angry.

Blue stood over the ball-human, guarding it. The Controller receded. The black blur swooped down and grabbed something shiny from the ground and brought it to the ball-human, who made noises and pressed the object to its eyes.

The Controller came forward inside Blue. Blue stepped off the ball-human toward the turtles and the siblings.

Blue fought, trying to move backward, tripping over the ball-human again and causing it to cry out.

Arrow Turtle pushed the new human aside. In the space between buildings, there was no safe place for the human to go. The Controller shoved Blue forward toward that turtle and the human-blob. This wasn't the turtle that had blasted Blue earlier, almost burning Blue to death.

Now, incredibly, the turtle pushed the human-blob toward Blue, nudging it with its big, wide arm. The human-blob showed no fear of the turtle. Blue wasn't an expert on human faces or emotions—humans had so few eyes, and their tiny flat mouths had less mobility compared to mandibles—but the human-blob seemed almost fond of the turtle. Humans were strange creatures.

The toggle switch moved inside of Blue's mandible. "Ana!" came the nonsense sound. "It's Mickey!"

The formerly running human ran again, straight toward Blue. The Arrow Turtle, seeming to see this with no eyes at all, rolled toward Squiggle and Slash. Inside the glass tunnel, the other human-blob had retreated all the way to the right. But the siblings kept smashing the gray glass. It glinted in the late afternoon sun, sprinkled across the ground and on the squishy bits that had been the fourth human blob.

The turtles roared and breathed fire on Slash and Squiggle.

Blue, horrified, immediately lunged forward to help its siblings, but the running human-blob, now still, grasped at its multipurpose appendage and held it back. The formerly running human-blob crouched beside the ball-human, opened its pack, and started wrapping the ball-human in white cloths, stopping the leaks.

The turtles tried to avoid running over the wet bits of the fourth human as they fought Squiggle and Slash, but Blue's siblings had no such qualms. And they were more nimble. Although the fire breath was devastating, it was difficult for the big, slow turtles, who could barely maneuver, to hit the smaller, quicker siblings.

Squiggle leaped onto Arrow Turtle's back. Blue approved. Round Turtle would not risk burning its own sibling. Slash came at Arrow Turtle from the side, trying to get just behind that large front arm, obviously looking for a way to dismantle it. From above, Squiggle held the arm in place, making it useless. Together, both spidogs were still smaller and lighter than Arrow Turtle, but they were annoying it.

The other turtle circled the scrum, searching for a weakness.

Blue leaned toward the fight, wanting desperately to help its siblings, even though its siblings had gone bad. The ball-human wrapped its weak hand around one of Blue's mismatched orange feet as if reading Blue's mind, keeping Blue there.

The flying black blur landed on Squiggle. Blue didn't like the flying thing. It reminded him of his sibling's eyes, but bigger and twistier. Speaking of eyes, the flying thing leaned over and somehow, using one of its appendages (a long, pointed thing), it started prying Squiggle's LED eyes right out of its head! Blue's mandibles fell open limply at the sight. Squiggle's multipurpose appendage tried to swat the flying thing off, but it simply levitated up and away from its reach each time and then landed and popped off another eye.

Blind, thrashing, Squiggle fell off the turtle. Arrow Turtle shook Slash loose from its arm and breathed a jet of fire onto it. Round Turtle moved in on the blind, helpless Squiggle and smashed the red-banded spidog with its oversized arm even as its sibling spat fire at it.

Squiggle was dying. Blue remembered dying. It had hurt. And Squiggle was dying blind in the darkness. But ball-human kept its weak grip on that mismatched orange foot, and somehow that was enough to keep Blue from throwing itself forward. The other human-blob was actually leaning on Blue, watching Squiggle die. That human-blob had no fear of Blue. The Controller held Blue back.

Blue rocked back and forth in distress, letting its blinking blue eyes send coded signals to its doomed sibling, signals Squiggle could not see.

The turtles destroyed Squiggle without finesse, smashing and burning, crushing and melting the spidog. Its crumpled white carapace darkened from the fire.

Although Blue strained with all its facilities, it could not tell when the life drained from Squiggle, when power stopped flowing through its crushed and melted circuits. The turtles did not stop pounding and burning the dirty white pieces that had been Squiggle until long after Squiggle could have fought back.

But everyone had forgotten Slash.

-32-
Mickey

Operating the blue spidog was exhilarating, as if Mickey's arm was another whole body. Or as if Ek had grown to an enormous size. But she was also limited, and it hurt her head, which felt as if it was on fire. Blue was stupid and stubborn. The range it could see was weird, with each eye attuned to a different visual spectrum, and its thoughts and understanding of what it saw were incredibly bizarre.

Mo was down, bleeding, badly injured, her plan to sneak past the spidogs an utter failure. The spidogs had slaughtered Persephone just like Doug, torn her apart. And now Ananda, for whatever reason, had wandered into the middle of a vicious five-way robot fight. Blue, even under Mickey's control, had no interest in shielding Ananda from the other spidogs and yearned to fight the Mind Melds.

"I'm going out there," Mickey said, leaving Blue to itself for a moment. Mo had hold of its leg, and its programming not to hurt people still seemed intact.

Across the space, the twins sat in their chairs, blinking headsets wrapped around their temples, controllers in hand, operating the Mind Melds, their faces scrunched in identical looks of concentration.

Emilio crouched beside Mickey, goggles on, watching the battle through Yellow's eyes. He pushed up the glasses, revealing his ashen face and reddened, wet eyes. Mickey realized he had been front and center to the awful dismemberment of Persephone. "No way. It's not safe."

Mickey brushed her hand across Pris's broken face. Pris stirred and blinked up at her. It appeared that Pris was trying to smile, but her battered lips could only grimace.

"I'll be okay, Emilio. Take care of Pris. Maybe she will adopt you."

"I'm not a baby. I'm just a little person."

"I know the difference." Obviously, he didn't know who Pris was. Probably that was best. "Sit here so she has a pillow."

Gingerly, she transferred her best friend's broken head to the acerbic robot jockey's lap. "If she starts talking about lawyers, that means she's feeling better." Mickey tried to joke, although she didn't think Pris could speak with her jaw like that. She touched Pris's short pink hair with her real fingers.

Pris blinked at her.

"I should have let you stay home." Mickey swallowed. Her two best friends were badly injured. And for what? Had anything Mickey had done over the last two days benefited anyone? What had they learned? That Mickey was a genetic freak. Useless knowledge.

Emilio curved one small hand on Pris's uninjured shoulder. The yellow controller lay abandoned on the floor. He grabbed Mickey with the other. His fingertips were calloused. "You're going to get hurt going out there."

"Haven't you heard, Emilio? I'm a freak. I'll be fine." She shook him off and picked her way through the crowd. Bao was arguing with Melody and a few other people. Melody had a spidog leg in her hand and was waving it.

The red lights on the walls flashed in time with the monotonous alarm. Someone needed to shut that down. It was making Mickey's neck hurt.

She should have told Taylor and Geoffrey where she was going, but they seemed busy kicking spidog ass outside, and anyway, they would see her soon enough through the Mind Melds. They wouldn't be happy.

She climbed through the spidog-size hole smashed through the door of the observation room. Once in the main hallway, she heard the fight. The breaking glass, the smashing metal.

The Mind Melds' treads had chewed up the yellowing grass around the robotics lab. Their trail was easy to follow. The ground was soft, muddy, and smelly from fallen, decaying leaves. No lights pulsed out here, but the alarms continued. Car alarms in the parking lot also blared, and several cars had roof and hood damage.

Mickey walked along the side of the robotics building, her arm almost touching it, trampling through some of the landscaping. Ek swooped to her side, landing on its spot on her shoulder, the bird's weight reassuring and familiar. She couldn't walk and control Blue at the same time, and she hoped Blue had stayed with Mo and out of the fight.

Ek would have recorded everything, which could be reviewed later. The raven rubbed its long beak against Mickey's ear and along the throbbing scar where the xoggotli had penetrated her neck. The scar was thick and hard since the xoggotli had gone deep before being turned into glass and extracted.

As Mickey neared the corner of the genetics building, the sounds of fighting increased—the noises of flamethrowers and crashing metal, of hydraulics. Mo's red sneakers, filthy with mud, sprawled on the ground. Mickey feared the worst, but Mo was still in them, wrapped in dirty, bloody gauze, holding onto one of Blue's legs with both hands. Blue was bouncing and swaying, leaning toward the Mind Melds, who had torn a spidog apart. One of the spidog legs had red paint on it—unless that was Persephone's blood.

Although Mickey had been inside Blue when Prime attacked earlier, the ferocity of the black robots frightened her. The Mind Melds, as far as she knew, had no autonomy at all. This was all Geoffrey and Taylor. It was one thing to see the big robots in the ring with other machines designed to fight each other. This was savage.

Mickey slipped around the edge of the building toward the hallway. Much of its glass was now on the ground, under and around the dwindling fight. She tried not to look at Persephone's muddy, ground-up remains. With the wall broken, Mickey could get inside and grab Aunt Lagatha. The two of them could retrieve Mo and retreat inside.

Aunt Lagatha shouted, "There's another one!" She waved both arms, her eyes wide and white.

Mickey used her prosthetic arm to clear shards of glass from the wall so it was easier to climb through. She assumed the woman was warning her about Blue, who was under control.

As she ducked to enter the hole, the other woman yelled again. "Ananda!"

Where was Ananda? She had run out a while ago after Mo, bandaged Mo up . . .

Ananda screamed.

-33-
Mickey

Aunt Lagatha raced from the end of the hallway to where Mickey stood with one foot inside and one outside. Ek ruffled its feathers and lifted from Mickey's shoulder as Aunt Lagatha grabbed Mickey's prosthetic arm so tightly that she almost yanked it off.

The Mind Melds stopped stomping the shattered spidog into the ground.

Blue pulled free from Mo's grasp and ran awkwardly along the side of the building, toward the animal lab.

"I told you there was another one!" Aunt Lagatha shook Mickey.

Mickey sucked in her cheeks. She couldn't believe she had forgotten that Ananda was outside, too. "I thought you meant Blue."

"I meant the third one, the yellow one."

The one Emilio was tracking, yes. The flashing lights and never-ending noise were eroding Mickey's thoughts.

Aunt Lagatha pulled at Mickey again. "Get in the hallway."

Mickey resisted, tugging the older woman outside. "I came to rescue you. Come on."

Prime and Alpha had swung their towers around and were trundling away in the direction of Ananda's screams.

"What about Ananda?"

As far as Mickey knew, Ananda was unhurt. Mo was badly injured, while Aunt Lagatha was just shaken up and angry. If only Blue hadn't run away. "Help Mo. Give me a moment."

Mickey leaned on the outside of the hallway, on a small section of unbroken smoked glass, and closed her eyes. She was still connected, faintly, to Blue. She reached down the thread to the spidog and tugged, trying to pull the spidog back.

-34-
Blue

Although the ball-human needed help, Slash seemed to need more help. Slash had found another human in need of rescue! The ball-human didn't seem capable of movement, so it would stay put. Plus, another human had already stopped the ball-human's leaks.

Blue shook its leg, dislodging the ball-human's grip, but gently, and trotted off to find Slash. A human was shouting from that direction, obviously for help. Two siblings would be better than one.

Deep in Blue's mind, the Controller fought for control. Blue did a little dance that shook its whole body as if to shake the Controller off. The directive was to save humans. One human's leaks were stopped, and it was firmly in place, unable to escape, and now Blue was off to save another. Blue was doing its job. The Controller was simply confused.

Plus, the turtles had killed Squiggle. Were still killing Squiggle, even though clearly Squiggle was very dead. Blue had to team up with Slash against the fierce turtles. Blue had not known the siblings could die, torn to bits like fragile people. What if the turtles turned on the humans?

Blue turned a corner and found Slash crammed into a concrete canyon with a human-shaped blob. The blob was trying to climb the canyon wall to a ledge, but Slash kept grabbing it with its multipurpose appendage and knocking it back to the concrete ground. Obviously, there was danger on the ledge, and Slash was saving the human-blob from going up there.

Slash was wise in the ways of human-blobs.

Blue saw steps leading to the ledge and scurried up them to get behind and above the human-blob, so when it attempted to climb up, Blue could push it down as Slash pulled it down. Teamwork. Blue felt very satisfied to be keeping the human-blob out of danger. The human-blob did not seem appreciative, but humans were difficult to understand sometimes.

Blue held down the human-blob's head effortlessly with one leg and studied the canyon ledge, which was attached to a building where a small human-sized door hung open slightly, leading inside. Blue sent a message to Slash that perhaps more humans in need of rescue were in the building. The protocol instructed that the siblings should check all buildings.

Even if the door had been closed and locked, Blue had lock picks and electronic bypass mechanisms built into its toes. Blue was a full-service search-and-rescue spidog, after all. Abandoning the human-blob to Slash, Blue opened the door. It entered a crowded room that had no life-blobs inside. On the other side of the room was another door, closed. Blue recognized the pad on the wall as a type of lock. The third toe it tried caused the lights to change colors and the door to click open.

Ah, this room was full of life-forms, small ones, all imprisoned. Agitated life-forms, jumping around inside boxes. Blue had hit the rescue jackpot. It recognized some of the shapes as the life-forms it hunted in the arena. Hunted? No, that wasn't the correct word. Anyway, Blue began tearing the cages apart and freeing all the small blobs. The doors behind it were still open, allowing the blobs to escape Outside.

Inside its circuits, the Controller raged. Why, when Blue was doing its job? Blue did not much like this Controller. None of its other Controllers had interfered with Blue's duties.

As the last life-forms finished fleeing, the Controller kept trying to exert control over Blue, aiming its attention toward yet another touchpad on the wall. The touchpad was something Blue could deal with, presenting the correct key-foot to the pad. The door beside this lock was glass and of a strange construction. Blue grasped the edge of the door with its multifunction appendage and pulled.

The door swung open, but another door followed it. Blue pulled that door, and the same thing happened. Dozens of doors, it seemed like, although Blue was not the best at counting. Blue could see through the glass into a hallway where a human in great distress stood, looking at another human who was Outside. Blue's long, low body design did not fit the upright looping door. Blue did not have shoulders to shrug or breath to sigh with, but it paused before assuming the exciting new ball position and flinging itself through several panes of door glass and into the hall.

The Controller made noises through Blue's speakers at the human, who stepped aside.

Blue paused. The human-blob seemed to need rescue, but the Controller was pushing Blue to keep going. The human Outside, who was not at all distressed, waved at Blue to *go, go*, down the hallway to another one of the strange doors. Blue unlocked the door because that was protocol, then rolled through all the panes.

Eureka. This room was full of human-blobs, all of which began acting agitated with joy upon being rescued by Blue, who was universally beloved.

The Controller forced more noises from Blue's speaker, and the humans inside the room rushed at Blue, pushing it aside, and exited through the many doors in a kind of loop, one human per door, to be united with the distressed human in the hall, where they all became agitated again, not understanding they were being rescued.

The Controller to get in charge of Blue, which Blue disliked, and made even more noises with Blue's speakers, most of which Blue could not understand. But the human-blobs understood, and they calmed down, lowering themselves to the floor of the hallway, not quite into the pleasing ball-form, but close enough.

Along one wall of the room was a puzzling structure, a long glass bin full of water. The water messed with Blue's sensors, but there seemed to be life-forms inside. Water rescue was something Blue and its siblings—sibling, now—had not yet perfected. Their carapaces were not sealed properly against liquids, and their sensors couldn't sense life signatures, heat, through deep water.

Blue stalked across the room and sank onto its many feet to stare through the glass into the water. A crowd of tiny life-forms stared back. They did not have heat signatures. Were they not alive? The little creatures of many colors had waving halos of feathers around their heads and curved mouths, something that usually meant Blue had accomplished a task properly.

Blue was unsure if they needed saving. The tiny life-forms were moving, so they must be alive. But they were not in any distress. Meanwhile, the large human-blobs were shaking and moving in ways that matched distress, according to Blue's database. The Controller was still making noises through Blue's speaker. It was annoying, and Blue searched for a way to turn the speaker off since there was no way to cut off the Controller's access.

-35-
Mickey

If the Unieda team could program electronic bypass mechanisms into the feet of the spidogs, why couldn't supervisors like Aunt Lagatha have them in their smartwatches, Mickey wondered, her eyes closed as she followed Blue through the genetics laboratory. Blue had left Yellow behind, harrying Ananda in the loading dock, and that would have to be dealt with soon, but Blue had also freed all the trapped scientists from the lab (and all the lab animals). Mickey didn't have the mental bandwidth to tell her friends operating the Mind Melds where their girlfriend had gone. Blue was getting more difficult to control, and that was taking everything she had. Ek had dropped off her bandwidth and left her shoulder.

Perhaps Emilio would think to tell Taylor or Geoffrey what was going on, since he was presumably still watching through Yellow's eyes and the three men were all in the same room.

The survivors from the genetics lab crowded around Aunt Lagatha, hugging her, some of them crying. They didn't know that Persephone was dead, Mickey realized; they were still crying over Doug. That seemed so long ago.

Blue crashed back through the rotating door, rolled down the hallway, and unfolded into its full spidery form just before hitting the assembled group. Everyone screamed and shoved down the hall toward the animal building.

Mickey started to push her voice through Blue and then realized she was physically standing right there. "It's okay. He's the good one!" she reiterated.

Aunt Lagatha was the only one who had stayed put, just opposite Mickey. She raised one graying eyebrow and gazed at Mickey with steady blue eyes.

"I'm controlling him." Which wasn't exactly the truth. "He let you out, right? He didn't hurt anyone. It was the other two, the red and yellow ones, that hurt people." And why was that happening?

The other lab workers stopped pushing and shoving and turned toward Mickey.

She addressed Aunt Lagatha. "Should I have Blue un-lock the other door toward the robotics building, or do you all want to come outside?"

Aunt Lagatha studied the trampled, sloppy pieces of Persephone and then beyond Mickey. Mickey wondered what the Mind Melds were doing behind her. She had known them since the beginning, and she wasn't fright-ened, but after today, others might not feel that way. She knew the brothers had both under total control—unlike Mickey with Blue—but the Mind Melds appeared much more frightening, hulking, jagged, spitting fire, made to crush other robots to dust.

Aunt Lagatha concluded, "I think we would rather stay inside."

Blue pulsed slightly up and down, like a dog wanting to play, in front of Aunt Lagatha. Mickey didn't know what the programming in Red and Yellow was like (or had been like, in the case of Red), but Blue wasn't malicious. Blue didn't feel emotions, just did what it was programmed to do. Something had obviously changed the programming of the other two that Blue thought of as its siblings.

Mickey pushed Blue to go carefully around the small huddle of people, back through the lab, and pick open the other keypad. Blue resisted, wanting to stay and "help" the humans. She inspected this waist-height white spider with its doglike personality. She understood why the robotics team had added the extra legs for stability, but the resulting spider shape was too scary. Most people disliked spiders or were frightened of them. The original concept of a robotic search-and-rescue *dog*, even with fewer legs and a total lack of arms, seemed better. A child trapped in rubble would welcome a robot that looked like a friendly dog coming to save them. Very few people saw a three-foot-tall spider with glowing eyes and thought, "That is friend-shaped, and it's going to help me."

Blue bounced and moved its multifunction limbs at Aunt Lagatha, trying to offer her help she didn't need. Aunt Lagatha backed away, almost stepping on Mickey, who ended up outside on the muddy, bad-smelling ground. She was afraid the odors were mostly coming from Perse-phone's bits.

Mickey nudged Blue away from the people it was so eager to save and toward the keypad, trying to get into its dim programming that doing *that* would help people. Being inside Blue made her head hurt, reminding her of when she had tried to control Ek plus two other AI ravens last summer when she was trying to save the mersharks from being blown up.

She wished she could connect to Ek at the same time, but it was too much for her to manage, even with the upgrades to both the bird and her neural net. They hadn't improved her brain and its direct implants, after all. She had absolutely no desire for more brain surgery, although, in the future, she probably wouldn't have a choice. Hopefully, in the far future; her implants were only a few years old.

Gazing over the puddle of Persephone, Mickey saw Mind Meld Prime, piloted by Geoffrey, idling not far away, guarding Mo, and Ek sat on the lifting arm, partially powered down. Alpha was not in sight; she hoped Taylor had sent it to rescue Ananda from Yellow at the loading dock.

"Shoo." Aunt Lagatha flapped her hands. "Mickey—"

Mickey turned back. Blue had decided that the keypad would not be helpful and was approaching the people again. If Blue had been an actual spider, she would have threatened it with a rolled-up newspaper. *Bad arachnid.*

She waved at Prime, a kind of "can you help me here?" gesture. Prime rolled forward a few inches toward Mo, who honestly looked terrible, and then rolled back as if to say, *I'm working over here.*

It seemed like hours since Red had killed Doug and injured Pris and the others. And still, no first-response vehicles had arrived. Mo claimed Dr. Lee had blocked calls to 911, but that seemed unreal and honestly too stupid for words.

Mickey leaned inside the corridor and stared at Blue. It occurred to her that Blue probably didn't know Mickey was the human operating it. Why should it? Mickey had never been to Unieda before yesterday and had never operated the spidogs before today. It didn't seem like its grasp of humans as individuals was very good.

"Aunt Lagatha, can you help Mo? It looks like she has a first aid kit. I'll wrangle Blue. Yellow is—" she didn't want to say "gone" because that wasn't correct. "—Not around."

The women switched places, and Mickey approached Blue, who was clicking its mandibles and multifunction appendages at the crowd. It was slightly scary. She wasn't entirely sure that the whole spidog wasn't electrified, especially since it was damaged, but she placed her metal hand on its smooth white back. It didn't respond. Why should it have touch sensors on its back? On the plus side, it didn't immediately electrocute her either.

Mickey shoved at the spidog. "Go that way." Although it was mostly long legs, its body was heavy.

Blue staggered and then righted itself and did a little tap-tappedy dance to turn in place and face Mickey, mandibles and multifunction appendages open.

"I'm not fighting you, you stupid spider. Just go through there and unlock the doors, would you?"

Click-click, went the mandibles.

"Yes, very scary, now go." She pushed with her mind and felt a sharp tug of pain. She had almost reached her limit. It was getting to be time to stick her head in an ice bucket.

She listened to Blue grumbling in its mind about saving the human-blobs as it tiptoed, tap-tap-tap, down the corridor toward the lab. Trying to keep some part of her engaged with the spidog, she turned to Aunt Lagatha. "Is there some kind of instant ice pack in that first aid kit? I really need something cold for my head."

Another lab worker had also gone outside, and both were fussing over Mo. Mo's beautiful braids were muddy and messed up, and that hurt Mickey to see. Her friend's brown eyes were half open, but Mickey couldn't tell if Mo was seeing her or not. This day had gone so very wrong. She rubbed her forehead with her real fingers, pulling the skin back and forth.

The other lab worker, a man in his mid-thirties, tossed a plastic packet at Mickey. She caught it effortlessly with her metal hand, read the directions with slit eyes, cracked it open against her metal palm, then lifted it to the back of her skull over the neural net and its burning connections. The temperature of her head seemed to drop ten degrees immediately. Mickey indulged in a full-body shiver of relief.

In the genetics lab, Blue lifted one of its feet and poked at the pad beside the revolving door leading to the corridor to the robotics lab. The flashing red light over the doorway pulsed unrelentingly. That wasn't helping the pain in Mickey's head, nor was the alarm, which had been blaring throughout the campus and probably down the street the entire time.

Blue obviously still didn't comprehend revolving doors. Once again, it started pulling the doors endlessly toward itself, trying to figure out how to get through, although its long, low spider body would not fit the vertical slots.

The rest of the genetics lab staff pushed against the door, heading toward the main building. She sent Blue to unlock the other end of the corridor for them as well; the people Blue was trying to save avoided the spidog, and Mickey felt almost bad for it. She called Blue back as soon as it unlocked that other door.

Once everyone was through, she headed outside to Aunt Lagatha and Mo. She sat on the filthy ground next to her wounded friend. Ek flapped from its perch on Prime to Mickey's shoulder. Mo moved her hand toward Mickey, who took it and laced their fingers together, light brown to medium brown. She had held too many hands attached to broken friends today.

-36-
Blue

The human-blobs had left Blue alone in the corridor, and the Controller had retreated a bit after sending a vague instruction: *come to me*. What did that mean? If the Controller was in a place, Blue did not know where that place was. Blue really wasn't even sure what the Controller *was*.

However, Blue remembered where Slash had been, with the human-blob back in the canyon. Perhaps Slash needed help to rescue that human still. Outside this corridor, some human-blobs were attending to the ball-blob. But those other human-blobs did not seem to need rescue, remarkably. The ball was no longer leaking, for instance—leaking humans always required help. Another human was in pieces, very leaky indeed, but beyond help. And Squiggle, dear sibling, was also in pieces, leaking quite a bit of odd black fluid.

No one had trained Blue to rescue other spidogs. People were right there, though, and could repair Squiggle when they were done with the ball-human. They could put the black stuff back inside Squiggle where it presumably belonged. Blue assumed some people had repaired Blue after the fight and the fire that had broken its leg, melted its insides and broken its feet, even though Blue had died for a while.

Blue tiptoed back down the corridor through broken glass and made itself into a ball to go back through the strange doors into the building where the long, low container of strange, cold life-forms was. As Blue tip-tapped through that room, it noticed that some of the little life-forms were the same shade of black as the fluid that had leaked from Squiggle, which was odd. Blue made its way down another corridor to the other room now empty of small life-forms, their containers still hanging open after Blue's rescue.

Outside the next doorway was the canyon, and there was Slash and the human-blob—and Arrow Turtle.

The human was down, although it wasn't leaking and had not assumed ball-form. Slash used several feet to hold the human in place and stood backed into the canyon, multifunction appendages raised and clicking, with mandibles also clicking.

Arrow Turtle was a short distance away, sitting there menacingly on its big, round, black rolling feet, its front leg up in the air, ready to crush Slash.

Blue immediately saw the problem. Arrow Turtle could not crush and maim Slash because Slash was standing over the human. By hurting Slash, Arrow Turtle would hurt the human.

If Blue interfered and saved the human, Arrow Turtle would attack Slash and rend Slash to pieces the way the two turtles had torn up Squiggle. If the human escaped under its own power, leaving Blue behind, Blue would also be at risk of Arrow destroying it. Blue was already weak from the fire that the turtle had rained on Blue earlier in the arena, and Blue couldn't run away with any alacrity because of the misfitting replacement leg and feet. Blue couldn't fight Arrow Turtle alone while Slash took the human away, and neither could Slash fight Arrow Turtle alone if Blue took the human away. It was a stalemate.

Arrow Turtle rolled forward and raised its front leg higher.

Blue remembered that it once knew how to fight and searched its programming. The fight sequences were there but grayed out. Blue could only search for life-forms in need of assistance and save them. It could not be a war dog or a guard dog. It could only be a search-and-rescue dog right now.

Blue jumped from the canyon ledge and landed too hard, with all its joints buckling. The human recoiled under Slash. Blue stumbled as the replacement limb gave out beneath it, going down on a couple of its knees. Slash glanced over and then focused back on Arrow Turtle.

Blue tugged on Slash's human-blob, trying to pull it away. The human fought, but that very action caused Slash's feet to slip off and free the human. Blue yanked it, even though clearly that distressed the human. But Blue forced the human to stand up and get behind both spidogs.

Arrow Turtle hesitated, and its arm lowered slightly. It rocked back and forth on its treads. It did not have a face, not the way the siblings did, but to Blue, it seemed as if the Arrow Turtle was focused on Slash, not Blue.

The human wailed loud sounds of distress. Blue shoved backward with one foot, pressing the noisy human against the canyon wall for its own protection. Blue backed up a step, keeping the human on the wall. That left Slash open to attack by Arrow Turtle.

Arrow Turtle rolled forward. Blue could see down its nose, where the fire roiled, ready to be snorted out all over Slash. The world was extremely loud. Inside Blue's head, the Controller was trying to take control again to get Blue to pull the screaming human out of the canyon, away from both Arrow Turtle and Slash. The screaming human was, of course, screaming. Arrow Turtle rumbled. Over everything shrieked the alarm that told the siblings that humans needed help wherever they could be found. Slash, nervous, was tapping all its pointed toes on the concrete ground. Inside the seams of its white carapace gleamed a rainbow of black oil.

Blue's databases were not segregated by war, rescue, or guard functions, so Blue could easily locate information on oil. Oil was flammable and could be used as a weapon.

Blue could not access protocols on how to use weapons. And this weapon was inside Slash, throughout Slash.

And Blue remembered vividly what it felt like to burn.

Arrow Turtle breathed fire onto Slash, and its heat bathed Blue. Shamefully, Blue tried to back away, stepping on the howling human. Blue did not want to burn again. The human's cries increased a notch. The Controller wrestled Blue for control.

Black oil from inside Slash oozed out of the cracks and crannies in its carapace as Arrow Turtle breathed loud, furious fire, bathing the yellow-and-white spidog from mandibles to toes.

The Controller tugged Blue sideways and forced Blue to drag the human along, keeping its fragile, soft body behind Blue's tough white exoskeleton. Although perhaps the Controller had forgotten, or didn't know, that a turtle had easily penetrated that carapace with fire earlier that day and that Blue was still broken from that attack.

Iridescent oil puddled around Slash's toes.

Blue shoved the human-blob into the far corner of the canyon. It continued to wail and began to beat on Blue's back. Blue lifted the new weird foot and placed it against the human's middle, not very nicely, and pressed firmly. The human stopped hitting Blue.

Arrow Turtle stopped breathing fire. Maybe it needed to cool down or inhale; Blue didn't know. Blue didn't breathe, after all.

The puddle around Slash spread. More oil came from Slash's joints. It did not drip or pour from the joints. It crept, very deliberately, down Slash's legs to join the inky pool.

Arrow Turtle swayed slightly back and forth before Slash, as if waiting to see what the yellow spidog would do.

The Controller tried to get Blue to lead the human away, but the oil's behavior fascinated Blue. It was the wrong temperature, for one thing. It should have been the same temperature as Slash, but it was slightly warmer. Was that from the fire?

Blue lifted one of its multipurpose appendages and inspected the spaces in its own joints. No oil. The human squeaked, and Blue backed into it, making it grunt.

The black puddle coalesced and moved toward Arrow Turtle. Slash seemed unaware of this odd action, but Blue leaned forward to observe. This allowed the human-blob to slip around it and dash away.

Arrow Turtle recoiled from Slash as the human darted by.

The puddle kept creeping toward Arrow Turtle, although the concrete ground sloped in the opposite direction. Blue sent a suggestion to Slash to back up, which the sibling did.

Just before the blackness would have touched Arrow Turtle, the big monster bot threw one last contemptuous gout of fire at Slash, wheeled around and followed the fleeing human.

The puddle drew in on itself and retreated inside Slash. Slash looked at Blue. Blue clacked its mandibles in confusion, having no shoulders to shrug.

Out in the grass, a small life-form hopped. Slash waved its multipurpose appendages gleefully and sprang into the air. Its white carapace had scorch marks, but its insides seemed undamaged from the fire. Slash landed on the life-form and grabbed it, flinging it high.

Blue was sure that life-form had been inside the build-ing a short time ago. Hadn't Blue just saved it? The Con-troller was telling Blue to take the small life-form away from Slash, but Slash was having so much fun—oh, there it went, pop. No more life-form. Oops.

Slash bounced away, chasing whatever small life-forms moved in the grass, its carapace scorched black and spat-tered red. Blue did not want to fight with Slash. Blue was tired.

Metal screeched as Slash threw itself on top of vehicles with glee. More loud sounds joined the cacophony. Blue took a few steps in that direction, but the strange leg gave out, and at the top of the ramp, Blue canted to one side. It pushed itself upright but immediately fell again, and some-thing loose inside fell off.

Blue was gone.

-37-
Mickey

Ananda, screaming, guarded by Mind Meld Alpha, ran around the corner of the building. Although terrified, she didn't seem injured.

Through a fading Blue, Mickey watched Yellow tear apart a white laboratory rabbit and then run into the parking lot to destroy more cars, setting off a volley of car alarms. A moment later, Blue went dark, and she lost contact.

Yellow rampaged through the lot toward the fence enclosing the Unieda campus. Mickey winced as Yellow trampled over Pris's car, which added its shrieks to the general noise level. Insurance companies in the Northeast were going to be very unhappy after today.

Aunt Lagatha gave Ananda a cursory check, but it was clear she hadn't been badly hurt, although she was holding both arms across her belly. The turrets of both Mind Melds swiveled between the activity beside the broken corridor, where Aunt Lagatha had returned to Mo's side, and watching Yellow, who was almost at the front gate.

Mickey wondered how long their batteries lasted. A Robo Rumble fight was five minutes long. The Mind Melds had been running for what seemed like hours, and their power had to be draining fast. The smaller, lighter spidogs could operate for longer periods of time, no matter what their current function was.

Mickey tried to connect to Blue, but there was nothing. Whatever had happened, Blue was offline.

Ananda looked at Mickey sideways and said rather loudly, "You can stop blaming me for losing the xoggotli now."

Mickey scrunched her face in disbelief and blinked at the non sequitur. Why was she bringing this up now?

On the ground, Mo waved her hand, but Mickey couldn't tell what she was trying to say.

"What?" Mickey said, annoyed, glancing away from Ananda at Yellow. That problem seemed a bit more pressing, as the spidog had reached the fence and seemed to contemplate climbing it.

"I saw it," Ananda declared. She wiped her face with the back of her hand.

"No," Mo groaned.

"Saw what?"

A police SUV pulled up to the guardhouse. Finally. The nasty, mean guard lady actually emerged to lean into the vehicle and talk to the officers.

Yellow crouched in a bush on the other side of the fence.

"The xoggotli, aren't you paying attention?" Ananda cried.

"We all saw it," Mickey replied. "And we lost every piece of it because you let go." She briefly touched her scar where the creature had been inside her.

"I saw it today," Ananda said just as the guard triggered the gate.

"What? Where?" Mickey looked away from the gate.

Mo's hand dropped back onto the damp ground, and Aunt Lagatha bent over her. They said something too low for Mickey to hear.

"Today, aren't you listening to me?"

"Here?" Mickey flashed a glance at the police vehicle as it rolled through the gate.

"In that horrible spider. The xoggotli came out of the spider when it was fighting Alpha and then crawled back in."

"That spider?" Mickey pointed at Yellow.

Yellow jumped onto the police SUV.

"Yes!"

The SUV stopped, and officers got out of both sides. Mickey ran.

-38-
Mickey

In hindsight, she probably could have grabbed one of the golf carts, but she didn't know how to operate them, so it wouldn't have saved time. Mickey ran across the damp, squishy lawn, ignoring the walkways, going straight as she could toward the police officers. Ek swooped before her.

Her head was pounding. She had dropped the ice pack. Noise emanated from every corner of the Unieda campus. The police unit's lights were flashing, the red and blue making purple, but thankfully, the siren was off.

The officers, both men, hadn't drawn their weapons. They seemed more curious than frightened by the large white robotic spider on their SUV's roof. The mean guard lady stood in the open gate, her hands over her mouth. Mickey wondered if she even knew what kind of hijinks happened inside the fence or if she was just paid to be obstructive and rude to people trying to get in.

Ek swooped down and tried to knock Yellow off the roof. Yellow swatted at the raven with both of its multipurpose appendages, scoring a lucky hit. Ek tumbled through the air and crashed into the windshield of a nearby car, setting off another alarm.

Stumbling, Mickey tried to connect to Yellow, but of course, Emilio was already in there. Maybe, given time, no headache, and no urgency, she could have ousted the little man and made her way in to control Yellow, but as things stood, there was no way. All she saw was seething blackness.

When she checked the police vehicle again, Yellow had jumped off toward the passenger side, on top of that hapless officer, and was embracing him with its multipurpose appendages. Mickey knew what came next, and she wanted to close her eyes, but she had to keep running. Maybe she could save the other cop. She hoped Mo wasn't watching; her stepdad was a police officer.

"Run!" Mickey shouted, but her breathing was ragged, and the autumn wind blew her words away.

The policeman popped.

The other officer clutched his radio, shouting into his shoulder, running around the front of the SUV, his gun in his other hand.

"Run away!" Mickey gasped.

Something big and hot approached behind Mickey and passed by. Mind Meld Prime. Geoffrey to the rescue.

Mickey stumbled to a stop as Prime, big and menacing, trundled through the lot toward the stopped police car. The surviving police officer had no way of knowing Prime was a good robot, just like he hadn't known that Yellow was bad.

She reached inside herself, dug the tips of her sneakers into the asphalt, and launched herself after Prime. Prime, being wide, had to take an indirect route, but she could run between cars.

Far off, sirens sounded, a lot of them. Dr. Lee was going to be pissed off. Maybe someone in a nearby industrial park had heard all the alarms and called it in despite his precautions.

"Get back in the car!" Mickey yelled at the officer.

Yellow was tearing up the first officer with what could only be described as glee. The second officer aimed his weapon at the spidog. Bullets ricocheted off the curved, reinforced body of the spidog back at the cop. One shot hit him in the leg.

Mickey groaned. More car alarms started as bullets slammed into vehicles.

The cop fell to one knee.

Yellow advanced, its filthy carapace only slightly dented, its mandibles clacking, multipurpose appendages raised and ready to grab.

Prime emerged from between two rows of cars and charged at Yellow, who recoiled. So did the officer. The officer shot reflexively at Prime, and again, the bullets failed to penetrate the thick metal armor. Prime tried to nudge the cop aside, but its big metal body had overheated from running for an extended time, and the officer took that as an attack.

Mickey shouted, "The black one is okay! Let it help you!"

The officer leaned away from Prime, his gun still raised. Yellow reached out with its multipurpose appendages to grasp the man. Mickey wanted to cover her eyes, but she kept running, although she knew that she would be too late.

Prime shoved the officer over, not at all gently, and smashed Yellow with its lifting arm. Yellow staggered, curled into a ball, and tried to roll away.

Ek darted down to land on the sprawled officer and raised its wings protectively. Mickey arrived a moment later, grabbed the man by his arm, and yanked at him. Although he was much bigger than Mickey, he slid easily through the gore of his former partner, groaning and swearing at her to let him go.

"Don't be an idiot," Mickey retorted. "I'm saving your stupid life here."

He still fought her.

Yellow tried to roll after them, but Prime smashed its lifting arm into the gore-caked ball of spidog again and again until the tough carapace cracked open, revealing the electronics and hydraulics inside.

And the iridescent black oil.

-39-
Mickey

Mickey splayed herself horribly on top of the wounded police officer to hold him back from fighting. She stared at the writhing blackness inside Yellow.

And the blackness stared back.

She rolled off the protesting cop and fell to her knees, her metal hand going to the scar on her neck as a sudden searing heat seemed to penetrate it.

The blackness shaped a bubbling bit of itself into an eye and gazed at Mickey. It blinked. She blinked back.

The moment seemed to last forever, but then Prime's arm smashed into Yellow again, destroying its components. Yellow's legs dropped limply. Although Mickey hadn't connected to Yellow, she felt it go out at the very edge of her consciousness.

The oil shifted, not at all dead. It blinked at her again.

No, it was winking.

How had the xoggotli gotten inside Yellow?

Fuck.

-40-
Mo

"Thank you for getting us adjoining rooms," Mo said to Pris.

Pris nodded. Doctors had wired her jaw shut, and half her face was bandaged after being rebuilt by the expert plastic surgeons at Yale-New Haven Hospital. She sat propped up in the hospital bed, her head shaved, even skinnier than usual, but Mo couldn't be mad at her for that.

Mo's arm was in a sling post-operation, and her whole middle was tightly wrapped. It hurt to breathe, talk, laugh, move and even eat—maybe she would lose a couple of pounds herself. She had a lot of physical therapy ahead of her; Mickey shared her physical therapist's information with Mo.

Pris used a stylus to write on a tablet suspended on a telescoping arm next to her bed. "No cameras," she wrote, followed by a sad face.

"Not that we could use the footage if we had it. Those spidogs are proprietary."

Pris drew another sad face.

"Hey, at least your fossils are going to be in the Peabody Museum. Dr. Lee is still paying for it, even after everything."

Pris shrugged one shoulder and then drew a sad face with Xs for eyes.

"Yeah, a lot of people died."

They stared at each other. Pris wore no makeup. Her eyelashes were pale, almost nonexistent, her lips a thin white line of pain. Her family was filming a new season of their reality show and had wanted to make Pris's near-death experience a centerpiece, but Pris had never been on the show and still refused.

Pris raised her hand slowly back to the tablet. Her brain had received quite a knocking, but the doctors were sure she would make a full recovery. "Xoggotli?"

Mo bit her lower lip. "Dr. Lee has it—them?—now. That's not good, of course. He's a fellow mad scientist, but I don't trust him." Visions of how the spidogs had acted when animated by the xoggotli would never leave her head. They assumed Red had been infected, too, but somehow Blue had not been.

"Mickey?" Pris wrote.

Mo shrugged. She hadn't been back to Unieda to finish her DNA work since that day. "I don't know. We never found any relatives of hers. She has some has some unusual DNA sequences in common with a couple of the mersharks but she's not a mershark."

"Human, right?" Pris wondered.

"I mean, yeah, she's human, of course."

"Who's human?" Mickey walked into the hospital room, Ek perched on her shoulder.

"You are, Mickey," Mo said.

"Course I am."

Mickey held out her right hand to Pris. She had a brand-new, picture-perfect tattoo of the black axolotl with the bifurcated tail on her forearm as if the creature was sitting there. Pris touched Mickey's fingers with her own and then pointed at the tattoo.

Mickey ran her metal fingers over it. "You wouldn't believe it if I told you."

Mo laughed. "Mickey, we recently saw giant metal spiders kill people. Of course, we will believe you."

"Right," Pris wrote.

"I visited that little axolotl I liked so much before I left Unieda that day," she said to Mo. Mickey turned to Pris. "They have a big tank of them in the genetics lab. The lab workers, specifically Ananda, cut them up while they are alive and torture them."

"That's not quite true—" Mo protested.

"Anyway, I wanted to see it one last time. It crawled out of the tank onto my arm just like this—" she pointed to the tattoo. "And then it, well, it melted into my arm and left this shadow."

"You're right, I don't believe it," Mo said. "But it's a good story to tell about your new tattoo."

Mickey cocked her head, leaning her cheek against Ek, and gazed at her two friends. "Why were you wondering if I was human when I walked in? Back to that stupid DNA test?"

Pris nodded.

"There's something else, though, that we didn't get to tell you yet that Aunt Lagatha and I found in your blood,"

Mo ventured. She reached out and ran her fingers over Mickey's new tattoo. The black was slightly iridescent and raised. She had never seen tattoo ink like that.

Mickey pulled her arm away.

"You know how there was a xoggotli inside Yellow, and probably inside Red, and they don't know how it got there? Pretty weird, of course."

Pris nodded and then put her hand to her bandaged cheek as if that hurt.

"Well, Aunt Lagatha and I were looking at your blood under a microscope right before everything went to hell that day, and we saw something. She's still trying to figure it out, but I think we know what it is, although we don't know what it means."

Mickey gazed at Mo. Her brown eyes seemed darker than ever before. Ek shifted on her shoulder.

"Mickey, your blood has tiny black globules in it."

Pris sucked in a loud breath. The stylus tap-tap-tapped on the screen scribbling furiously, but Mo didn't look away from Mickey.

"Mickey, the xoggotli is in you."

###

Equipment Malfunction Kills Three at Local Biotech Firm

Malfunctioning equipment at Unieda Corporation yesterday tragically killed two employees and a first responder and injured a dozen people. The same malfunction prevented employees from notifying emergency services. Help only arrived hours later after neighboring businesses complained to the police about continuous alarms coming from the Unieda campus. Dr. Bao Lee, Chief Medical Officer, alleges industrial espionage by a rival firm. Employees of that rival company were also on the Unieda campus yesterday on what was scheduled to be a collaborative visit . . .

The Woman with No Relatives, an Anomalous mtDNA Case Study

By Dr. Lagatha Larsen, Dr. Ananda Patel, Dr. Melissa McLeod, et al.

Abstract: A 28-year-old woman, Jane Doe, exhibits mtDNA that doesn't match any known lineage. Her immediate relatives are unknown as she was abandoned at birth . . .

###

About the Author

Gevera Bert Piedmont is a neurodivergent cyborg swamp witch living on the edge of a frog pond in Connecticut with her spouse, cats, and an impressive collection of rubber lizards. She is the author of The Maw and Other Time-Traveling Lizard Tales, the Mickey Crow paranormal series, co-author of Airesford (the other author is an actual zombie), editor of the Necronomi-RomCom Cthulhu Mythos duology and Amazon bestselling co-editor of Horror Over the Handlebars, an anthology of Connecticut horror. Her next anthology, with co-editor Elizabeth Davis of Dead Fish books, will be The Atlas of Deep Ones.

Her novel Fat Monster will be published by Nightmare Press in late 2024.

Bert has an MFA in creative writing and belongs to HWA, Connecticut Authors and Publishers Association, and New England Horror Writers. Her (very) small press publishing company is Transformations by Obsidian Butterfly, LLC, and at this time is only publishing anthologies. Connect at Facebook.com/geverabertpiedmont, geverabertpiedmont. com, obsidianbutterfly.com, or her Amazon and Goodreads author pages.

She loves hearing from fans.

Facebook.com/geverabertpiedmont

https://linktr.ee/bybertabird for all author pages and other social media links

Please leave a review on Amazon and/or Goodreads, and follow Bert on both. Authors live on reviews and coffee, and Bert doesn't drink coffee. Thank you!